拜倫詩選／

漫步在美的光影

She Walks in Beauty

中·英對照雙語版

喬治·戈登·拜倫——著

陳 金——譯

笛藤出版

前　言

　　唯美詩化的文字，猶如夜幕蒼穹中的密佈星羅，自悠久的歷史長河之中散發出璀璨迷人的耀目光環，是人類精神世界中無價的瑰寶。千百年來，由各種文字所組成的篇章，經由傳遞淬煉，使其在各種文學彙集而成的花園中不斷綻放出絢幻之花，讓人們沉浸於美好的閱讀時光。

　　作者們以凝練的語言、鮮明的節奏，反映著世界萬象的生活樣貌，並以各種形式向世人展現他們內心豐富多彩的情感世界。每個民族、地域的文化都有其精妙之處，西洋文學往往直接抒發作者的思想，愛、自由、和平，言盡而意亦盡，毫無造作之感。

　　18 ～ 19 世紀，西洋文學的發展進入彰顯浪漫主義色彩的時期。所謂浪漫主義，就是用熱情奔放的言辭、絢麗多彩的想像與直白誇張的表現手法，直接抒發出作者對理想世界熱切追求與渴望的情感。《世界經典文學 中英對照》系列，精選了浪漫主義時期一些作者們的代表作，包括泰戈爾的《新月集》、《漂鳥集》；雪萊的《西風頌》；濟慈的《夜鶯頌》；拜倫的《漫步在美的光影》；葉慈的《塵世玫瑰》。讓喜文之人盡情地徜徉於優美的文字間，領略作者及作品的無盡風采，享受藝術與美的洗禮。本系列所精選出的作品在世界文學領域中皆為經典名作，因此特別附上英文，方便讀者對照賞析英文詩意之美，並可同時提升英文閱讀與寫作素養。

在這一系列叢書當中，有對自然的禮讚，有對愛與和平的歌頌，有對孩童時代的讚美，也有對人生哲理的警示。作者們在其一生中經歷了數次變革，以文字的形式
寫下了無數天真、優美、現實、或悲哀的篇章，以無限的情懷吸引著所有各國藝文人士。文學界的名人郭沫若與冰心便是因受到了泰戈爾這位偉大的印度著名詩人所著詩歌的影響，在一段時期內寫出了很多類似的詩作。在世界文學界諸多名人當中有貴族、政治名人、社會名流、也有普羅大眾，他們來自不同的國家、種族，無論一生平順或是坎坷，但其所創作品無一不是充滿了對世間的熱愛，對未來美好世界的無限嚮往。

編按：由於經過時間變遷、地域上的區別，許多遣辭用句也多所改變，為期望能更貼近現代讀者，特將原譯文經過潤飾，希望讀者能以貼近生活的語詞，欣賞濟慈所欲傳達的詩意哲理。

| 目　錄 |

當初我倆分別／

當初我倆分別，
只有沉默和眼淚，
心兒幾乎要破碎，
得分隔多少年歲；
你的臉蒼白又冰涼，
你的吻更寒意逼人，
那一刻正預示了
我今日的悲傷。

那天冰冷的朝露
滴在我的額頭，
它似乎警示了
我此刻的痛楚。
你背棄了所有的誓言，
名聲也輕飄似雲。
聽到別人提起你的名字，
我也感到無地自容。

When We Two Parted

When we two parted

In silence and tears,

Half broken-hearted

To sever for years,

Pale grew thy cheek and cold,

Colder thy kiss;

Truly that hour foretold

Sorrow to this!

The dew of the morning

Sunk chill on my brow—

It felt like the warning

Of what I feel now.

Thy vows are all broken,

And light is thy fame:

I hear thy name spoken,

And share in its shame.

他們在我面前提到你，

一聲聲如同喪鐘敲響在耳際；

我渾身顫慄——

為什麼對你如此深情？

沒人知道我瞭解你，

太過瞭解了——

我將長久地為你懊悔，

懊悔之深難以言述。

我倆祕密地相會，

我獨自神傷，

你的心兒竟忘卻，

你的靈魂竟欺騙。

如果多年以後，

我們再見面，

我該怎樣面對你？

只有沉默和眼淚。

They name thee before me,

A knell to mine ear;

A shudder comes o'er me-

Why wert thou so dear?

They know not I knew thee

Who knew thee too well:

long, long shall I rue thee,

Too deeply to tell.

In secret we met-

In silence I grieve,

That thy heart could forget,

Thy spirit deceive.

If I should meet thee

After long years,

How should I greet thee?

With silence and tears.

雅典的女郎 ╱

趁我們還沒分手的時光,

還我的心來,雅典的女郎!

不必了,心既已離開我胸膛,

你就留著吧,把別的也拿走!

請聽我臨別的誓言:

你是我的生命,我愛你。

憑著你那些鬆散的髮辮,

愛琴海的清風將它們眷戀;

憑著你長長睫毛的眼睛,

親吻你那嫣紅的臉頰;

憑著那野鹿般的眼睛發誓:

你是我的生命,我愛你。

Maid of Athens, Ere We Part

Maid of Athens, ere we part,

Give, oh, give back my heart!

Or, since that has left my breast,

Keep it now, and take the rest!

Hear my vow before I go,

My life, I Love you.

By those tresses unconfined,

Wooed by each Aegean wind;

By those lids whose jetty fringe

Kiss thy soft cheeks' blooming tinge;

By those wild eyes like the roe,

My life, I Love you.

憑著我癡情渴慕的紅唇，

憑著那絲帶緊束的腰身，

憑著這些定情的鮮花告訴你，

它們勝過一切言語的表達；

憑著愛情的歡樂和酸辛對你說：

你是我的生命，我愛你。

我走了，雅典的女郎，

懷念我吧，在孤寂的時光！

雖然我已飛往伊斯坦布爾，

我的心兒和靈魂卻留在了雅典：

我能夠停止愛你嗎？不能！

你是我的生命，我愛你。

By that lip I long to taste;

By that zone-encircled waist;

By all the token-flowers that tell

What words can never speak so well;

By love's alternate joy and woe,

My life, I Love you.

Maid of Athens! I am gone:

Think of me, sweet! when alone.

Though I fly to Istambol,

Athens holds my heart and soul:

Can I cease to love thee? No!

My life, I Love you.

只要再克制一下／

只要再克制一下，我就會解脫於

這內心陣陣撕裂的痛苦；

最後一次向你和愛情長歎，

我就要重回忙碌的人生。

如今的我，隨遇而安，混著日子，

卻未曾讓我歡喜；

縱使世間的樂趣都已消逝，

還有什麼悲傷能讓我心酸？

拿酒來吧，再擺上筵席，

人不適合孤獨地生存於世；

我要做個無情的浪蕩子弟，

隨眾人歡笑，不為他人悲慟。

在美好的日子裡我不會這樣，

我永遠不會這樣，但是你

逝去了，留下我孤獨地在這裡；

沒有你──一切都沒有意義。

One Struggle More, and I Am Free

One struggle more, and I am free

From pangs that rend my heart in twain;

One last long sigh to love and thee,

Then back to busy life again.

It suits me well to mingle now

With things that never pleased before!

Though every joy is fled below,

What future grief can touch me more?

Then bring me wine, the banquet bring;

Man was not form'd to live alone:

I'll be that light, unmeaning thing

That smiles with all, and weeps with none.

It was not thus in days more dear,

It never would have been, but thou

Hast fled, and left me lonely here;

Thou 'rt nothing—all are nothing now.

我的豎琴不能瀟灑地彈唱！

「憂傷」勉強露出的笑容

就像石墓上的玫瑰花，

嘲諷著隱藏著的悲哀。

雖然有快樂的同伴和我共飲，

可以暫時驅散滿腹的鬱怨；

雖然快樂將發瘋的靈魂點燃，

這顆心啊──這顆心依然孤獨！

多少次，在寂靜清幽的夜晚，

我欣慰地凝望蒼穹，

我猜想，天上的光芒

正甜甜地照射你沉思的眼睛；

我常想，在新西雅的正午，

當船在愛琴海的波濤中行駛，

我會想：「塞莎正在仰望那輪明月」

唉，月光在她的墓上閃耀！

In vain my lyre would lightly breathe!

The smile that sorrow fain would wear

But mocks the woe that lurks beneath,

Like roses o'er a sepulchre.

Though gay companions o'er the bowl

Dispel awhile the sense of ill :

Though pleasure fires the maddening soul,

The heart, - the heart is lonely still!

On many a lone and lovely night

It sooth'd to gaze upon the sky;

For then I deem'd the heavenly light

Shone sweetly on thy pensive eye:

And oft I thought at Cynthia's noon,

When sailing o'er the Aegear wave,

" Now Thyrza gazes on that moon " -

Alas, it gleam'd upon her grave!

當我因病痛在失眠的床上輾轉時，

病痛正抽搐著我那跳動的血管，

「塞莎不會懂得我的痛苦，」

我虛弱地說：「這也是一種安慰。」

就像被折磨一生的奴隸，

給他自由並無裨益，

悲慈的造物主徒給我生命，

因為，塞莎已經與世長辭！

那時塞莎美好的誓言，

生命和愛情還依然新鮮！

啊，這與如今的你是多麼不同！

歲月給你度上了怎樣的愁暈！

那和你一起許給我的心

沉默了──唉，願我的心也沉默！

雖然它冷若逝人，

卻還能感到，它厭惡那寒氣。

When stretch'd on fever's sleepless bed,

And sickness shrunk my throbbing veins,

"T is comfort still," I faintly said,

"That Thyrza cannot know my pains: "

Like freedom to the time-worn slave,

A boon 'tis idle then to give,

Relenting Nature vainly gave

My life, when Thyrza ceased to live!

My Thyrza's pledge in better days,

When love and life alike were new!

How different now thou meet'st my gaze!

How tinged by time with sorrow's hue!

The heart that gave itself with thee

Is silent — ah, were mine as still!

Though cold as e'en the dead can be,

It feels, it sickens with the chill.

你那心酸的信物！你淒哀的紀念！

雖然令人心痛，卻依然緊貼於我的胸前！

請繼續保存那份愛情，讓它長久，

否則就打破你那緊貼的心。

時間只能將愛情凝固，卻不能移動，

希望的破滅會讓愛情更加神聖。

啊，千萬顆跳動的愛心又怎能

比得上這對逝者的鍾情？

Thou bitter pledge ! thou mournful token!

Though painful, welcome to my breast!

Still, still preserve that love unbroken,

Or break the heart to which thou'rt press'd.

Time tempers love, but not removes,

More hallow'd when its hope is fled:

Oh !what are thousand living loves

To that which cannot quit the dead?

無痛而終 ╱

時間遲早都會帶來

使死者平靜的無夢的睡眠。

遺忘吧！希望你倦怠的翅膀

輕輕揮舞在我將臨終的榻前！

不要讓一群朋友和繼承人

哭泣，或者盼望，我即將的死亡；

不要讓披頭散髮的少女

感受或佯裝，適度地悲傷。

Euthanasia

When Time, or soon or late, shall bring

The dreamless sleep that lulls the dead,

Oblivion! may thy languid wing

Wave gently o'er my dying bed!

No band of friends or heirs be there,

To weep, or wish, the coming blow:

No maiden, with dishevelled hair,

To feel, or feign, decorous woe.

讓我靜靜地沉入泥土，
不要讓多事的憑弔者接近我，
我不想破壞他人片刻的歡樂，
也不願用眼淚驚嚇友情。

愛情，如果在臨終的時刻，
能夠止住無益的歎息，
對生的她，和死的他，
也許能施展最後的魔力。

But silent let me sink to earth,

With no officious mourners near:

I would not mar one hour of mirth,

Nor startle friendship with a tear.

Yet Love, if Love in such an hour

Could nobly check its useless sighs,

Might then exert its latest power

In her who lives, and him who dies.

你死了 ╱

我的賽琪！但願到最後
仍能看到你依舊恬靜的容顏。
忘記過去的鬥爭，
苦痛本身也會對你微笑。

但這願望已是徒然——因為美麗
會消逝，就像那微弱的呼吸，
女人那易流出的淚水，
生時欺騙你，死時哀悼你。

And Thou Art Dead, as Young and Fair

'Twere sweet, my Psyche! to the last

Thy features still serene to see:

Forgetful of its struggles past,

E'en Pain itself should smile on thee.

But vain the wish — for Beauty still

Will shrink, as shrinks the ebbing breath;

And women's tears, produced at will,

Deceive in life, unman in death.

讓我在最後的時刻孤獨地離去，

沒有遺憾，沒有呻吟，

沒遭受許多人遭到的死神貶低，

痛苦轉瞬即逝，甚至不會被察覺。

「唉，但是死了，去了。」 啊！

去所有人必須要去的地方！

重回到我生前的虛無，

再也沒有生命和活著的哀傷！

想想你曾經歡愉的時光，

算算你沒有痛苦的日子，

你就知道了，無論你曾經如何，

還是化作虛無最好。

Then lonely be my latest hour,

Without regret, without a groan;

For thousands Death hath ceas'd to lower,

And pain been transient or unknown.

"Ay, but to die, and go," alas!

Where all have gone, and all must go!

To be the nothing that I was

Ere born to life and living woe!

Count o'er the joys thine hours have seen,

Count o'er thy days from anguish free,

And know, whatever thou hast been,

'Tis something better not to be.

你死了，如此年輕、漂亮，

沒有人比得上你；

你嬌柔、絕美的面容

這麼快就歸於泥土！

雖然泥土將你納入了懷中，

而人們也將不經意地或歡喜地

踏踩在那上面，

只有一個人絕不會忍心

注視你的墳墓片刻。

我不會問，你長眠在哪裡，

也不會長久地注視那墳塚，

讓野花雜草在那裡盡情蔓延吧，

我不願看見。

夠了，我已經知道

我的所愛，我心上的人

竟會和泥土一樣腐蝕；

墓碑無需給我指出，

我一直深愛的竟是虛無。

And thou art dead, as young and fair

As aught of mortal birth;

And form so soft, and charms so rare,

Too soon return'd to Earth!

Though Earth receiv'd them in her bed,

And o'er the spot the crowd may tread

In carelessness or mirth,

There is an eye which could not brook

A moment on that grave to look.

I will not ask where thou liest low,

Nor gaze upon the spot;

There flowers or weeds at will may grow,

So I behold them not:

It is enough for me to prove

That what I lov'd, and long must love,

Like common earth can rot;

To me there needs no stone to tell,

'T is Nothing that I lov'd so well.

但我卻愛你到最後，

如同你愛我那般狂熱；

你對我始終忠貞不渝，

現在更不該改變。

愛情被死亡封鎖，

歲月不會將它冷卻，

情敵也無法將它偷走，

負心又能被抹掉；

遺憾的是，你看不到

我的過失、錯誤或改變。

Yet did I love thee to the last

As fervently as thou,

Who didst not change through all the past,

And canst not alter now.

The love where Death has set his seal,

Nor age can chill, nor rival steal,

Nor falsehood disavow:

And, what were worse, thou canst not see

Or wrong, or change, or fault in me.

我們曾度過美好的時光，

現在苦時只有我一人承受；

歡愉的太陽、兇險的風暴，

再不會是你的所有。

你那無夢之眠的靜寂，

我已羨慕得不再哭泣；

而我也不再抱怨

你的美麗已隨你而去，

我原會看著它日漸暗淡。

開得最嬌豔的花朵，

必然最先凋落；

而花瓣，縱然沒有手去摘取，

也會隨時間凋殘；

然而，看花兒朵朵凋零，葉兒片片落下，

比看它今日突然被摘去

更讓人心痛；因為人的眼睛怎堪接受由美變醜的過程。

The better days of life were ours;

The worst can be but mine:

The sun that cheers, the storm that lowers,

Shall never more be thine.

The silence of that dreamless sleep

I envy now too much to weep;

Nor need I to repine

That all those charms have pass'd away,

I might have watch'd through long decay.

The flower in ripen'd bloom unmatch'd

Must fall the earliest prey;

Though by no hand untimely snatch'd,

The leaves must drop away:

And yet it were a greater grief

To watch it withering, leaf by leaf,

Than see it pluck'd to-day;

Since earthly eye but ill can bear

To trace the change to foul from fair.

不知我能否忍受

親眼看著你的美貌漸漸消失，

清晨過後的夜晚

一定更顯陰暗。

無雲的白晝過去了，

而你直到臨終都那麼迷人，

去了，卻不凋零；

你好似劃過夜幕的星星，

在沉落時最為耀眼。

如果我可以像以前那樣哭泣，

我真該好好哭一場，

想到在臨終的床前，

我不曾有一夜的守護；

不曾憐愛地注視你的臉，

不曾輕輕地擁你入懷，

不曾支撐著你越來越低垂的頭；

我該表示我的愛，無論多麼徒勞，

啊，這種愛我們已不能再體會。

I know not if I could have borne

To see thy beauties fade;

The night that follow'd such a morn

Had worn a deeper shade:

Thy day without a cloud hath pass'd,

And thou wert lovely to the last,

Extinguish'd, not decay'd;

As stars that shoot along the sky

Shine brightest as they fall from high.

As once I wept, if I could weep,

My tears might well be shed,

To think I was not near to keep

One vigil o'er thy bed;

To gaze, how fondly! on thy face,

To fold thee in a faint embrace,

Uphold thy drooping head;

And show that love, however vain,

Nor thou nor I can feel again.

可是，你留下的珍異，

儘管都由我拾取，

我仍得不到多少依舊可愛的東西，

還不如就這樣把你存留於記憶！

通過陰森可怕的永恆，

你那永不凋謝的一切

會伴我重生；

但你深埋的愛最可親——

勝過一切，除了它活著的時辰。

Yet how much less it were to gain,

Though thou hast left me free,

The loveliest things that still remain,

Than thus remember thee!

The all of thine that cannot die

Through dark and dread Eternity

Returns again to me,

And more thy buried love endears

Than aught except its living years.

漫步在美的光影 ╱

I

她漫步在美的光影，像夜晚

皎潔無雲，繁星滿天；

明與暗最美妙的色澤

在她的容顏和明眸裡呈現：

耀眼的白晝只嫌光太強，

因它比那光亮柔和且舒適。

II

增一分陰暗或少一絲光明

都會傷及這難言的美。

美蕩漾在她的黑髮間，

或輕柔地照亮她的臉龐

在那臉龐，恬靜的思緒甜美地表達著

它的來處多麼純潔而珍貴。

She Walks in Beauty

I

She walks in beauty, like the night

Of cloudless climes and starry skies;

And all that's best of dark and bright

Meet in her aspect and her eyes:

Thus mellow'd to that tender light

Which heaven to gaudy day denies.

II

One shade the more, one ray the less,

Had half impair'd the nameless grace

Which waves in every raven tress,

Or softly lightens o'er her face;

Where thoughts serenely sweet express

How pure, how dear their dwelling-place.

III

啊，那面頰，那額際，

如此溫和，如此沉靜，又脈脈含情，

那迷人的微笑，那容顏的光彩，

都在訴說與人為善的時光：

她與世無爭，

內心卻充溢著純真的愛！

III

And on that cheek, and o'er that brow,

So soft, so calm, yet eloquent,

The smiles that win, the tints that glow,

But tell of days in goodness spent,

A mind at peace with all below,

A heart whose love is innocent!

我的心漆黑一片 ╱

I

我的心靈漆黑一片——哦，快點

彈奏我還能忍受的豎琴，

用你溫柔的手指，

在我耳邊低語，如此銷魂。

假如這顆心仍把希望珍藏，

這音樂會讓它著迷得訴說衷情：

假如這眼睛裡還隱含著淚花，

它會流出來，不再讓我的頭腦焦灼。

My Soul Is Dark

I

My soul is dark-Oh! quickly string

The harp I yet can brook to hear;

And let thy gentle fingers fling

Its melting murmurs o'er mine ear.

It in this heart a hope be dear,

That sound shall charm it forth again;

It in these eyes there lurk a tear,

'T will flow and cease to burn my brain.

II

但求你的樂聲粗獷而深沉，

不要先彈出歡樂的旋律，

告訴你，歌者啊，我必須哭泣，

否則我沉重的心就會爆裂；

因為它曾經浸透了太多的憂傷，

又在無眠的靜寂裡痛得久長。

如今它註定要受到最重的一擊，

或者立刻破裂——或者皈依歡聲歌唱。

II

But bid the strain be wild and deep

Nor let thy notes of joy be first:

I tell thee, minstrel, I must weep,

Or else this heavy heart will burst;

For it hath been by sorrow nursed

And ached in sleepless silence long;

And now 'tis doomed to know the worst,

And break at once or yield to song.

我看過你哭 ╱

I

我看過你哭——一大顆晶瑩的淚珠

湧上你藍色的眼眸；

我心想，這多麼像

紫羅蘭上青翠欲滴的露珠；

我看過你笑——藍寶石的火焰

在你面前也黯然失色；

啊，寶石的閃爍怎麼比得上

你那一瞥放出的光彩。

I Saw Thee Weep

I

I saw thee weep-the big bright tear

Came o'er that eye of blue;

And then me thought it did appear

A violet dropping dew:

I saw thee smile-the sapphire's blaze

Beside thee ceased to shine;

It could not match the living rays

That filled that glance of thine.

II

猶如烏雲從遠方的太陽

得到了濃厚而柔和的色彩，

就連黃昏的暗影

也不能從天上將其驅趕；

你的笑容給我陰鬱的腦中

注入了聖潔的歡笑；

你陽光般的笑容留下一道光芒，

照亮我的內心。

II

As clouds from yonder sun receive

A deep and mellow dye,

Which scarce the shade of coming eve

Can banish from the sky,

Those smiles unto the moodiest mind

Their own pure joy impart;

Their sunshine leaves a glow behind

That lightens o'er the heart.

樂章 ／

沒有一個美的女兒

像你那樣充滿魅力；

對於我，你甜蜜的聲音

猶如音樂飄浮水面：

仿佛那聲音攏住了

沉醉的海洋，使它停歇，

海面風平浪靜，波光粼粼，

風也好似在夢中流淌。

午夜的月光正在編織

波濤上明亮的珠鏈；

海的胸膛輕輕起伏，

恰似嬰兒的睡眠。

我的心靈向你臣服，

側耳聆聽，欽慕有加：

就像夏季海洋的浪潮

充滿溫柔。

Stanzas for Music

There be none of Beauty's daughters

With a magic like thee;

And like music on the waters

Is thy sweet voice to me:

When, as if its sound were causing

The charmed ocean's pausing,

The waves lie still and gleaming,

And the lulled winds seem dreaming;

And the midnight moon is weaving

Her bright chain o'er the deep,

Whose breast is gently heaving

As an infant's asleep:

So the spirit bows before thee,

To listen and adore thee,

With a full but soft emotion,

Like the swell of summer's ocean.

普羅米修斯 ╱

I

巨人！以你不朽的眼睛看來

塵世所受的苦痛

是可悲的現實，

並不該被眾神蔑視，

但你的悲憫得到什麼回報？

是默默的痛苦，愈來愈烈；

是面對岩石、餓鷹和枷鎖，

是只有高傲的人才能感知的痛苦，

還有他不想透露的心酸。

那鬱積胸中的一段苦情，

它只能在孤獨時吐露，

即便那時，也得小心，

天上有誰聽見，更不能歎息，

除非它沒有回音。

Prometheus

I

Titan! to whose immortal eyes

The sufferings of mortality

Seen in their sad reality,

Were not as things that gods despise;

What was thy pity's recompense?

A silent suffering, and intense;

The rock, the vulture, and the chain,

All that the proud can feel of pain,

The agony they do not show,

The suffocating sense of woe,

Which speaks but in its loneliness,

And then is jealous lest the sky

Should have a listener, nor will sigh

Until its voice is echoless.

II

巨人！你註定要

掙扎於痛苦和意志之間，

雖不致死，卻要歷盡磨難；

而那冷酷無情的上天，

那飛揚跋扈的宿命，

那一意孤行的「憎恨」，

它為了歡愉創造出萬物，

然後又把眾生一一毀滅，

甚至不讓你以死解脫；

永恆——這不幸的天賜

是你的，而你卻善於忍受。

司雷的大神逼出了你什麼？

只有你對他的一句詛咒，

你所承受的折磨也會砸在他身。

II

Titan! to thee the strife was given

Between the suffering and the will,

Which torture where they cannot kill;

And the inexorable Heaven,

And the deaf tyranny of Fate,

The ruling principle of Hate.

Which for its pleasure doth create

The things it may annihilate,

Refused thee even the boon to die:

The wretched gift eternity

Was thine-and thou hast borne it well.

All that the Thunderer wrung from thee

Was but the menace which flung back

On him the torments of thy rack;

你能夠推知未來的命運，

卻不肯說出以求和解；

你的沉默成了他的判決，

他的靈魂徒勞地悔恨；

邪惡的恐怖已無法掩飾，

瞧，他手中的閃電正在顫慄。

III

你神聖的罪行是心懷慈悲，

你要以你的教訓

減輕人間的不幸，

並振奮起人類自強的意志；

儘管上天蓄意和你為敵，

但你仍然抗爭至今，

你那堅不可摧的靈魂，

那來自天上和人間的暴風雨

又怎能摧毀你的堅忍和勇敢！

你給了我們有力的教訓：

The fate thou didst so well foresee,

But would not to appease him tell;

And in thy Silence was his Sentence,

And in his Soul a vain repentance,

And evil dread so ill dissembled

That in his hand the lightnings trembled.

III

Thy Godlike crime was to be kind,

To render with thy precepts less

The sum of human wretchedness,

And strengthen Man with his own mind;

But baffled as thou wert from high,

Still in thy patient energy,

In the endurance, and repulse

Of thine impenetrable spirit,

Which Earth and Heaven could not convulse,

A mighty lesson we inherit:

你是一個表徵，一個標記，

象徵著人類的命運和力量；

和你一樣，人也有神的一半，

煩惱的河流來自聖潔的源頭；

人也能預見一部分

自己悲慘的宿命；

他的苦痛，他的頑強，

和他生存的孤立無援：

但這一切反而令他奮起，

並喚起他頑抗的精神，

使他與不幸相持。

堅定的意志，深刻的感受，

即使在痛苦中，他能看到

其中也有它凝聚的回報。

勝利不在話下，

呵，死亡就是勝利。

Thou art a symbol and a sign

To mortals of their fate and force;

Like thee, Man is in part divine,

A troubled stream from a pure source;

And Man in portions can foresee

His own funereal destiny;

His wretchedness, and his resistance,

And his sad unallied existence:

To which his Spirit may oppose

Itself-and equal to all woes,

And a firm will, and a deep sense,

Which even in torture can descry

Its own concenter'd recompense,

Triumphant where it dares defy,

And making Death a Victory.

好吧，我們不再一起漫遊 ／

好吧，我們不再一起漫遊，

消磨這漫漫黑夜，

儘管這顆心仍然流淌著愛情，

儘管月光依舊皎潔。

因為劍已無法插進劍鞘，

靈魂也不再甘於狹小的胸膛，

這顆心啊，它要停下來呼吸，

愛情也需要歇息。

雖然夜晚為愛情而降臨，

白晝卻又會很快到來，

在這月色皎潔的夜晚，

我們已不再一起漫遊。

So, We'll Go No More A Roving

So, we'll go no more a roving

So late into the night,

Though the heart still be as loving,

And the moon still be as bright.

For the sword outwears its sheath,

And the soul outwears the breast,

And the heart must pause to breathe,

And love itself have rest.

Though the night was made for loving,

And the day returns too soon,

Yet we'll go no more a roving

By the light of the moon.

致湯瑪斯‧摩爾 ╱

I
我的小船靠在岸邊，

我的大船停在海上，

但在離去之前，湯瑪斯‧摩爾啊，

祝你健健康康！

II
向愛我的人致以歎息，

向恨我的人還以微笑，

無論頭頂的天空是陰是晴，

我都準備接受命運的挑戰。

To Thomas Moore

I

My boat is on the shore,

And my bark is on the sea;

But, before I go, Tom Moore,

Here's a double health to thee!

II

Here's a sigh to those who love me,

And a smile to those who hate;

And, whatever sky's above me,

Here's a heart for every fate.

III

儘管海洋在我身邊咆哮，

它仍會載我前行；

儘管沙漠將我包圍，

仍舊可能覓得甘泉。

IV

當我在井邊乾渴難耐，

如果井底只剩下一滴水，

在暈倒前，我仍要

為你的健康飲下它。

V

如同現在的這杯酒，

我會一飲而盡：

祝你我的靈魂安寧，

湯瑪斯·摩爾啊，祝你健康！

III

Though the ocean roar around me,

Yet it still shall bear me on;

Though a desert should surround me,

It hath springs that may be won.

IV

Were't the last drop in the well,

As I gasp'd upon the brink,

Ere my fainting spirit fell,

'Tis to thee that I would drink.

V

With that water,as this wine,

The libation I would pour

Should be-peace with thine and mine,

And a health to thee,Tom Moore.

寫於佛羅倫斯至比薩途中 ╱

哦，不要和我談論故事中的偉大人物，
我們年輕的時光就是我們的輝煌歲月；
在甜蜜二十二歲上的常春藤和桃金娘
比得上你所有的榮譽，不管它們開得多茂盛。

比起佈滿皺紋的額頭，花冠和王冕又算得了什麼？
那不過是凋零的花朵灑上了五月的朝露。
不如把這一切從蒼白的頭上拿走，
只散發光彩的花環又何足牽掛？

Stanzas Written on the Road Between Florence and Pisa

Oh, talk not to me of a name great in story;

The days of our youth are the days of our glory;

And the myrtle and ivy of sweet two-and-twenty

Are worth all your laurels, though ever so plenty.

What are garlands and crowns to the brow that is wrinkled?

'Tis but as a dead flower with May-dew besprinkled:

Then away with all such from the head that is hoary!

What care I for the wreaths that can only give glory?

啊，美名！如果我也曾因你的讚譽感到欣喜，

那不止是你富麗堂皇的辭句，

而是想看到親愛的人兒用她那雙明亮眼眸去發現，

我這愛她的人並非等閒之輩。

因此，我才追尋你，也只有我能發現你。

她的目光是籠罩著你的最美的光線，

聽到我講的精彩故事，她都會眨著大眼睛，

我知道那就是愛，我認為那才是榮耀。

O Fame!-If I e'er took delight in thy praises,

'Twas less for the sake of thy high-sounding phrases,

Than to see the bright eyes of the dear one discover

She thought that I was not unworthy to love her.

There chiefly I sought thee, there only I found thee;

Her glance was the best of the rays that surround thee;

When it sparkled o'er aught that was bright in my story,

I knew it was love, and I felt it was glory.

今天我三十六歲／

是時候了，這顆心應該平靜如水，
既然它已不再打動人心；
可是，儘管我不能為人所愛，
我還要去愛別人！

我的日子飄零在枯葉裡，
愛情的花朵與果實都已不再，
只剩下蛀蟲、災禍和悲痛
還緊纏我身！

那鬱積在我內心的火焰
就像一座孤寂的火山島，
這烈焰點燃的不是火炬——
而是，火葬堆！

On This Day I Complete My Thirty-sixth Year

'Tis time this heart should be unmoved,

Since others it hath ceased to move:

Yet, though I cannot be beloved,

Still let me love!

My days are in the yellow leaf;

The flowers and fruits of love are gone;

The worm, the canker, and the grief,

Are mine alone!

The fire that on my bosom preys

Is lone as some volcanic isle;

No torch is kindled at its blaze-

A funeral pile!

希望、恐懼、嫉妒的關照，
那部分崇高且折磨的
愛情的力量，我都不曾品嚐，
除了它的鎖鏈。

啊，為何在此時、此地，
讓這種思緒折磨我的靈魂；
榮譽正裝飾著英雄的屍架，
花環正點綴著他的額頭。

看！刀劍、軍旗、戰場，
榮譽和希臘，將我包圍！
那由盾牌抬回的斯巴達人
何曾有過這種自由。

The hope, the fear, the jealous care,

The exalted portion of the pain

And power of love, I cannot share,

But wear the chain.

But 'tis not thus-and 'tis not here-

Such thoughts should shake my soul, nor now,

Where glory decks the hero's bier,

Or binds his brow.

The sword, the banner, and the field,

Glory and Greece, around me see!

The Spartan, borne upon his shield,

Was not more free.

醒醒！（不，希臘已經覺醒！）
醒來，我的靈魂！想一想
你的心血所遭受的磨難，
還不快快刺進敵人的胸膛！

踏滅那復燃的情欲吧，
沒出息的成年！你應該對
美人的顰笑
不屑一顧。

如果你對青春抱憾，又何必苟活？
使你光榮而死的國土
就在這裡——去到戰場上，
獻出你的生命吧！

尋找一個不易被發現的歸宿吧，
士兵的墓地對你最適宜；
環顧四周，選一方風土，
靜靜地安息。

Awake! (not Greece-she is awake!)

Awake, my spirit! Think through whom

Thy life-blood tracks its parent lake,

And then strike home!

Tread those reviving passions down,

Unworthy manhood!-unto thee

Indifferent should the smile or frown

Of beauty be.

If thou regret'st thy youth, why live?

The land of honourable death

Is here:-up to the field, and give

Away thy breath!

Seek out —less often sought than found-

A soldier's grave, for thee the best;

Then look around, and choose thy ground,

And take thy rest.

在巴比倫的河畔我們坐下來哭泣／

I

我們在巴比倫的河畔坐下來

哀傷地哭泣，想到那天

我們的敵人如何在屠戮叫囂中，

焚毀了撒冷高聳的神殿；

而你們，她淒慘的女兒！

都號哭著四處逃散。

II

當我們憂鬱地凝視河流

看河水在腳下自由地流淌，

他們命令我們歌唱。呵，絕不！

我們絕不讓他們得逞！

寧可讓這只右手永遠枯瘦，

也不用我們的聖琴為敵人彈奏！

By the Rivers of Babylon We Sat Down and Wept

I

We sat down and wept by the waters

Of Babel, and thought of the day

When our foe, in the hue of his slaughters,

Made Salem's high places his prey;

And ye, oh her desolate daughters!

Were scattered all weeping away.

II

While sadly we gazed on the river

Which rolled on in freedom below,

They demanded the song; but, oh never

That triumph the stranger shall know!

May this right hand be withered for ever,

Ere it string our high harp for the foe!

III

我將豎琴掛在柳梢，

噢，撒冷！它的歌聲應該是自由的。

你輝煌盡失的時刻，

卻把你的遺物留給我：

呵，我永遠不會讓這悠揚的曲調

和暴虐者的聲音混在一起！

III

On the willow that harp is suspended,

Oh Salem! its sound should be free;

And the hour when thy glories were ended

But left me that token of thee:

And ne'er shall its soft tones be blended

With the voice of the spoiler by me!

詠錫雍 ∕

自由意志的永恆精神！
自由啊，你在地獄中最為珍貴！
因為在那裡你存在於人的心中——
那心啊，只聽命於你的愛情。
當信徒們被帶上枷鎖，
犧牲在那潮濕、暗無天日的地獄中，
他們的祖國也因這些烈士而受人尊敬，
自由的聲譽隨風傳播。

錫雍！你的監獄成了一方聖土，
你陰鬱的地面也成了神壇，
因為伯尼瓦爾在那裡邁步
留下深深的印記，仿佛你冰涼的石板
是長草的泥土！也許沒人將印記抹去
因為它們在暴政下向上帝控訴。

Sonnet on Chillon

Eternal Spirit of the chainless Mind!

Brightest in dungeons, Liberty! thou art,

For there thy habitation is the heart-

The heart which love of thee alone can bind;

And when thy sons to fetters are consign'd-

To fetters, and the damp vault's dayless gloom,

Their country conquers with their martyrdom,

And Freedom's fame finds wings on every wind.

Chillon! thy prison is a holy place,

And thy sad floor an altar-fort' was trod,

Until his very steps have left a trace

Worn, as if thy cold pavement were a sod,

By Bonnivard!May none those marks efface!

For they appeal from tyranny to God.

寫給奧古斯塔 ╱

當周圍開始變得陰暗，
理性也偷偷地收起了光線，
只有希望泛出微弱的火光，
我在歧途上孤獨前行。

在思緒紛飛的午夜時分，
內心開始激烈的鬥爭；
摧殘被稱作仁慈。
軟弱者絕望，冷漠者離去。

逢命運逆轉，愛情逃離，
憤恨之矢萬箭齊發，
你是我唯一的星光，
高懸天穹，永不隕落。

Stanzas to Augusta

When all around grew drear and dark,

And reason half withheld her ray-

And hope but shed a dying spark

Which more misled my lonely way;

In that deep midnight of the mind,

And that internal strife of heart,

When dreading to be deemed too kind,

The weak despair-the cold depart;

When fortune changed-and love fled far,

And hatred's shaft flew thick and fast,

Thou wert the solitary star

Which rose and set not to the last.

啊，幸有你長明不晦的光芒，
像天使的眼睛，守護著我，
永遠閃爍著憐愛的光芒，
為我阻擋黑夜。

當烏雲遮住頭頂，
試圖掩卻你的熠熠光芒，
而你遠布的光輝卻愈加純淨，
將周遭的黑暗盡行逐退。

願你的心向我心停靠，
告訴我何時當勇敢，何時當寬容。
你一句輕柔低語便可抵消
我所受的一切指控。

你好似一棵秀麗的樹，
高傲地挺立，卻微微俯首，
樹葉婆娑，忠誠、慈愛，
為你深愛的故物遮風擋雨。

Oh ! blest be thine unbroken light !

That watched me as a seraph's eye,

And stood between me and the night,

For ever shining sweetly nigh.

And when the cloud upon us came,

Which strove to blacken o'er thy ray-

Then purer spread its gentle flame,

And dashed the darkness all away.

Still may thy spirit dwell on mine,

And teach it what to brave or brook-

There's more in one soft word of thine

Than in the world's defied rebuke.

Thou stood'st as stands a lovely tree,

That still unbroke, though gently bent,

Still waves with fond fidelity

Its boughs above a monument.

狂風將襲，暴雨將至，
在風雨最虐之時，
你依然熱切溫存，
哀泣的綠葉灑遍我周身。

無論我的命運如何，
我決不讓你遭受厄運；
陽光普照的天國會獎賞
仁者──你當之無愧！

與褪色的愛情絕交吧，
只有你的情誼永世難消；
你的心靈善感，卻始終不渝，
你的靈魂柔順，卻巍然屹立。

當一切都失去，
唯有你不變，
你博大的胸襟一直向我敞開，
世界不再是荒漠──對我也不例外！

The winds might rend-the skies might pour,

But there thou wert-and still wouldst be

Devoted in the stormiest hour

To shed thy weeping leaves o'er me.

But thou and thine shall know no blight,

Whatever fate on me may fall;

For Heaven in sunshine will requite

The kind-and thee the most of all.

Then let the ties of baffled love

Be broken-thine will never break;

Thy heart can feel-but will not move;

Thy soul, though soft, will never shake.

And these, when all was lost beside,

Were found and still are fixed in thee;-

And bearing still a breast so tried,

Earth is no desert-ev'n to me.

失眠人的太陽 ／

啊，失眠人的太陽！憂鬱的星！

宛如淚珠，從遠處泛出光明點點

只能說明你驅不走的黑暗，

多麼像歡樂追憶在心坎！

「過去」那往日的明輝仍在閃爍，

光線微弱，溫存全無；

「憂傷」如一線光明盡在瞭望黑夜，

它清晰，卻遙遠；燦爛，卻又多麼寒冷！

Sun of the Sleepless

Sun of the sleepless! melancholy star!

Whose tearful beam glows tremulously far,

That show'st the darkness thou canst not dispel,

How like art thou to joy remember'd well!

So gleams the past, the light of other days,

Which shines, but warms not with its powerless rays;

A night-beam sorrow watcheth to behold,

Distinct but distant-clear-but, oh how cold!

我送你的項鍊 ／

送你的項鍊玲瓏精緻，
我贈你的詩琴悅耳動聽；
向你奉獻的心兒也忠誠，
誰知卻碰上了命運的不公。

兩件禮物都有奇異的法力，
能知曉獨處的你是否忠誠；
它們的責任已盡——可惜
沒能教會你如何盡責。

項鍊環環相扣，結實無比，
但它禁不起生人的撫弄；
琴聲也悅耳——但莫相信
在別人手裡它同樣甜美。

The Chain I Gave

The chain I gave was fair to view,

The lute I added sweet in sound;

The heart that offer'd both was true,

And ill deserved the fate it found.

These gifts were charm'd by secret spell,

Thy truth in absence to divine;

And they have done their duty well,-

Alas !They could not teach thee thine.

That chain was firm in every link,

But not to bear a stranger's touch;

That lute was sweet-till thou could'st think

In other hands its notes were such.

只要他摘，項鍊就會折斷，

只要他彈，琴就啞口不言；

就讓他

換新的鏈扣，上新的琴弦吧。

你變的時候，它們也在變；

項鍊斷裂，琴聲喑然。

算了！和它們、和你說再見──

脆鏈、啞琴、背叛的心靈！

Let him who from thy neck unbound

The chain which shiver'd in his grasp,

Who saw that lute refuse to sound,

Restring the chords, renew the clasp.

When thou wert changed, they alter'd too;

The chain is broke, the music mute.

'Tis past-to them and thee adieu-

False heart, frail chain, and silent lute.

盧德派之歌 ╱

海外自由的遊子

付出了多少鮮血，才換來了自由；

若不能自由地生，我們寧願在戰鬥中死去！

我們要把所有國王都推翻！

除了我們的盧德王。

當布匹織畢，

梭子換成利劍，

我們要將這裏屍布，

狠狠扔向腳下的暴君，

讓它浸透血漿。

那顏色和他的心一樣黑，

因為他的血管早已爛如泥土；

然而這甘露，

可讓盧德所栽培的自由常青樹，

重新煥發生機！

Song for the Luddites

As the liberty lads o'er the sea

Bought their freedom, and cheaply, with blood,

So we, boys, we

Will die fighting, or live free,

And down with all kings but King Ludd!

When the web that we weave is complete,

And the shuttle exchanged for the sword,

We will fling the winding sheet

O'er the despot at our feet,

And dye it deep in the gore he has poured.

Though black as his heart its hue,

Since his veins are corrupted to mud,

Yet this is the dew

Which the tree shall renew

Of Liberty, planted by Ludd!

悼瑪格麗特表妹 ╱

晚風已無聲，夜色也已沉寂，
林間不曾有一絲微風穿梭。
我歸來祭掃瑪格麗特的墳墓，
把鮮花撒向這方我深愛的塵土。

這狹小墓穴裡歇息著她的身軀，
這身軀當年可是芳華乍吐，活力四射；
如今恐怖的死神已將她擄去，
美德和麗質也未能挽回她的生命。

哦！只要死神懂得一點點憐惜，
只要上蒼能撤銷命運的可怕裁決！
弔唁者就無需來這吐露悲思，
詩人也無需來這稱讚她的高潔。

On the Death of a Young Lady, Cousin to the Author

Hush'd are the winds, and still the evening gloom,

Not e'en a zephyr wanders through the grove,

Whilst I return to view my Margaret's tomb,

And scatter flowers on the dust I love.

Within this narrow cell reclines her clay,

That clay where once such animation beam'd;

The king of terrors seiz'd her as his prey,

Not worth, nor beauty, have her life redeem'd.

Oh !could that king of terrors pity feel,

Or Heaven reverse the dread decree of fate,

Not here the mourner would his grief reveal,

Not here the muse her virtues would relate.

為什麼要悲慟？她無比的靈魂正在高翔，

將沖出光芒萬丈的天宇；

垂淚的天使帶她到天國的閨房，

那兒，人間的善行將換來無盡的歡樂。

可否允許放肆的凡夫責問上蒼，

如癡似狂地斥責神聖的天意？

不！這愚妄的企圖已離我遠去，

我絕不會違逆我們的上帝！

回憶她的美德是這樣親切，

回想她的嬌容是這樣鮮活；

它們依舊能喚起我深情的淚花，

依舊盤亙在它們慣往的心田。

But wherefore weep !her matchless spirit soars,

Beyond where splendid shines the orb of day,

And weeping angels lead her to those bowers,

Where endless pleasures virtuous deeds repay.

And shall presumptuous mortals Heaven arraign!

And madly God-like Providence accuse!

Ah ! no far fly from me attemps so vain,

I'll ne'er submission to my God refuse.

Yet is remembrance of those virtues dear,

Yet fresh the memory of that beauteous face;

Still they call forth my warm affection's tear,

Still in my heart retain their wonted place.

自然的慰藉 ╱

群山聳立的地方，必有他的知音；

海濤翻滾的地方，是他棲身之所；

哪裡天空蔚藍，陽光明媚，

他就會興致勃勃，精力充沛在那漫步；

沙漠、森林、岩洞、浪花

都對他有深情厚誼；

他們互通語言，表達比他本土的書冊

更加清晰，他便常常拋開書卷

打開那湖光所映照的大自然的書頁。

Canto the Third

Where rose the mountains, there to him were friends;

Where rolled the ocean, thereon was his home;

Where a blue sky, and glowing clime, extends,

He had the passion and the power to roam;

The desert, forest, cavern, breaker's foam,

Were unto him companionship; they spake

A mutual language, clearer than the tome

Of his land's tongue, which he would oft forsake

For nature's pages glassed by sunbeams on the lake.

有如一個占卜者，他會觀望著繁星，

直到那裡也有如星光般

燦爛的生命；世俗，和世俗的紛爭

還有人性的弱點，此時全部置之腦後。

啊，那時如果他能帶著靈魂高翔，

他一定樂意；但這身軀會拽沉

永恆的火花，嫉妒它升起的光芒，

仿佛要割斷這唯一的聯繫：

它讓我們聯想到那遙遠的蒼穹。

然而在人類的居所，他卻成了這樣一個物什，

一刻不停，憔悴不堪，無精打采，不苟言笑，

沮喪得像一隻割斷翅膀的野鷹，

對於他，只有無邊無際的宇宙方可安身；

以後他又會一陣發狂，

有如籠子裡的小鳥，

用嘴和胸脯不斷去撞擊那鐵絲的牢籠，

直到全身羽毛都被鮮血染紅，就這樣，

他那被阻的靈魂憤熱咬噬著他的心胸。

Like the Chaldean, he could watch the stars,

Till he had peopled them with beings bright

As their own beams; and earth, and earth-born jars,

And human frailties, were forgotten quite:

Could he have kept his spirit to that flight,

He had been happy; but this clay will sink

Its spark immortal, envying it the light

To which it mounts, as if to break the link

That keeps us from yon heaven which woos us to its brink.

But in Man's dwellings he became a thing

Restless and worn, and stern and wearisome,

Drooped as a wild-born falcon with clipt wing,

To whom the boundless air alone were home:

Then came his fit again, which to o'ercome,

As eagerly the barred-up bird will beat

His breast and beak against his wiry dome

Till the blood tinge his plumage, so the heat

Of his impeded soul would through his bosom eat.

紐芬蘭犬墓誌銘 ╱

世之驕子行將歸塵，

雖無榮譽，卻門第顯赫；

名家雕刻昭示著葬禮之盛，

墓室圖像彰顯了逝者之功；

一切告妥，墓地所見，

盡是虛誇，本樣全無。

何如斯犬，忠貞不二，

主人還家，趨前迎候；

挺身衛主，忠心可鑒，

全心為主，勞頓求活；

死得卑微，卻不為人知，

天國之門向它關閉，

而人類——愚妄的蟲蟻！只圖免罪，

欲獨佔天堂，排斥異族。

Inscription on the Monument of a Newfoundland Dog

When some proud son of man returns to earth,

Unknown to glory, but upheld by birth,

The sculptor's art exhausts the pomp of woe,

And storied urns record who rest below:

When all is done, upon the tomb is seen,

Not what he was, but what he should have been:

But the poor dog, in life the firmest friend,

The first to welcome, foremost to defend,

Whose honest heart is still his master's own,

Who labours, fights, lives, breathes for him alone,

Unhonour'd falls, unnoticed all his worth-

Denied in heaven the soul he held on earth:

While Man, vain insect! hopes to be forgiven,

And claims himself a sole exclusive Heaven.

人類啊！你這孱弱之徒！

權力將你腐蝕，奴役更使你卑微；

若看透了你，便會鄙棄你，離開你——

生命如塵，墮落的東西！

淫欲的愛情，欺詐的友誼，

偽善的笑容，欺誑的言語！

你本性奸邪，卻冠冕堂皇，

相較牲畜，你真該羞愧。

見此荒塚，請君走遠——

爾輩所悼之人與此無緣。

謹立此碑，以志吾友：

今生我唯一的朋友——在此安息。

Oh Man! thou feeble tenant of an hour,

Debased by slavery, or corrupt by power,

Who knows thee well must quit thee with disgust,

Degraded mass of animated dust!

Thy love is lust, thy friendship all a cheat,

Thy smiles hypocrisy, thy words deceit!

By nature vile, ennobled but by name,

Each kindred brute might bid thee blush for shame.

Ye! who perchance behold this simple urn,

Pass on-it honours none you wish to mourn:

To mark a friend's remains these stones arise;

I never knew but one, -and here he lies.

寫給羅馬 ╱

羅馬啊，我的祖國！人類靈魂的聖城！

心靈的孤兒們必將來投奔你，

故國淒涼的母親！

在他們幾近窒息的胸中灑下淡淡的憂鬱。

我們的悲傷和痛苦又算得了什麼？來吧，

看這柏樹，聽這梟鳴，

獨自彷徨在破落的宮宇和皇位的階梯上，怎麼！

他們的煩惱僅是一瞬的悲涼——

我們腳下的世界，脆若泥土。

To Romance

Oh Rome! my country! city of the soul!

The orphans of the heart must turn to thee,

Lone mother of dead empires! and control

In their shut breasts their petty misery.

What are our woes and sufferance? come and see

The cypress, hear the owl, and plod your way

O'er steps of broken thrones and temples, Ye!

Whose agonies are evils of day-

A world is at our feet as fragile as our clay.

萬邦的尼奧比！站在廢墟中，

沒有王冠，沒有兒女，暗自神傷；

空的屍灰甌她枯枝般的手中攢緊，

那神聖的灰塵早已隨風飄散。

西庇阿的墓穴中早已散去，

那些屹立的石墓，也已倒塌；

英雄們在此長眠，啊，古老的台伯河！

你是否要奔流於大理石的荒原中？

揚起你黃色的波濤，淹沒她的哀愁。

The Niobe of nations! there she stands,

Childless and crownless, in her voiceless woe;

An empty urn within her wither'd hands,

Whose holy dust was scatter'd long ago;

The Scipios' tomb contains no ashes now;

The very sepulchres lie tenantless

Of their heroic dwellers: dost thou flow,

Old Tiber! through a marble wilderness?

Rise, with thy yellow waves, and mantle her distress.

孤獨 ╱

獨自坐在山岩上，對著河水和沼澤冥想，

或是緩緩地尋覓樹林遮蔽的景致，

走進那人跡罕至之地，

與自然界的萬物共同生活在一起，

或是攀登那陡峭、幽絕的山峰。

與荒原中的禽獸一同

獨倚在崖邊，看傾瀉的飛瀑──

這樣並不孤獨；僅僅是與自然的美麗

一次會晤，並打開她的寶藏流覽。

Solitude

To sit on rocks, to muse o'er flood and fell,

To slowly trace the forest's shady scene,

Where things that own not man's dominion dwell,

And mortal foot hath ne'er or rarely been;

To climb the trackless mountain all unseen,

With the wild flock that never needs a fold;

Alone o'er steeps and foaming falls to lean;

This is not solitude, 'tis but to hold

Converse with Nature's charms, and view her stores unrolled.

然而，倘若是在喧囂嘈雜的人群中，

去聽，去看，去感受，一心想獲取財富，

變成一個疲憊的流浪者，隨波逐流，

就不會有人祝福我們，我們也無人可祝福，

到處遍是不能患難與共的奴僕！

人們都在奉承、追隨、鑽營和祈求，

雖在知覺上我們是同族，

但若我們死了，臉上的笑容也不會有所收斂：

這就是舉目無親；啊，這就是孤獨！

But midst the crowd, the hurry, the shock of men,

To hear, to see, to feel and to possess,

And roam alone, the world's tired denizen,

With none who bless us, none whom we can bless;

Minions of splendour shrinking from distress!

None that, with kindred consciousness endued,

If we were not, would seem to smile the less

Of all the flattered, followed, sought and sued;

This is to be alone; this, this is solitude!

美麗的希臘 ╱

美麗的希臘！曾經輝煌而今衰敗的遺跡！

消逝了，卻永遠被記住；傾圮了，卻永遠偉大！

現在，誰能去喚醒你那沒落的子孫，

引領他們去砸爛那禁錮他們已久的枷鎖？

曾幾何時，你的子孫並非如此，

他們──絕望的勇士在等待著命運的召喚，

守望在荒涼如墓的海峽裡。

啊，有誰能重新燃起那勇敢的精神之火，

從尤斯塔斯河岸躍起，將你從墳墓中喚醒？

Fair Greece

Fair Greece! sad relic of departed worth!

Immortal, though no more; though fallen, great!

Who now shall lead thy scattered children forth,

And long accustomed bondage uncreate?

Not such thy sons who whilome did await,

The hopeless warriors of a willing doom,

In bleak Thermopylae's sepulchral strait-

Oh, who that gallant spirit shall resume,

Leap from Eurotas' banks, and call thee from the tomb?

啊，自由的精靈！想那年，在伐裡的山嵋，

當你和特拉希比洛斯隊伍在一起時，

你可曾預見今日，在愛梯克平原，

一連串陰鬱日子蒙蔽了綠野的美麗？

現在，不是三十個暴君來加固鎖鏈，

而是每個蠻人都在你的土地上肆無忌憚；

你的子孫們並沒有反抗，徒剩抱怨，

當土耳其人揮舞著鞭子，他們驚恐、戰慄，

他們一生都被奴役，話語行動失掉了勇氣。

除了外表，一切均已改變！

只要看著每雙眼睛閃爍的火星，

沒有人否認他們的胸中又重新燃燒起火焰，

你不滅的光輝，啊，久別的自由精靈！

眾人皆在昏睡：他們還不知道

那光復先祖河山的時刻已經來臨，

他們在盼望外面的援助並因此而歎息，

卻無膽量孤軍抵禦敵人的侵襲，

或者在奴隸的悲慘史上洗去自己的汙名。

Spirit of Freedom! when on Phyle's brow

Thou sat'st with Thrasybulus and his train,

Couldst thou forbode the dismal hour which now

Dims the green beauties of thine Attic plain?

Not thirty tyrants now enforce the chain,

But every carle can lord it o'er thy land;

Nor rise thy sons, but idly rail in vain,

Trembling beneath the scourge of Turkish hand,

From birth till death enslaved; in word, in deed, unmanned.

In all save form alone, how changed! and who

That marks the fire still sparkling in each eye,

Who would but deem their bosom burned anew

With thy unquenched beam, lost Liberty!

And many dream withal the hour is nigh

That gives them back their fathers' heritage:

For foreign arms and aid they fondly sigh,

Nor solely dare encounter hostile rage,

Or tear their name defiled from Slavery's mournful page.

世代被奴役的人們！你們可曾知道
要想獲得自由，就必須起來戰鬥！
要想取得勝利，就必須伸出自己的右手！
高盧或莫斯科能救你們嗎？不能！
當然，他們也許能擊潰你們的勁敵，
然而卻不是為了你們，而為自由的神壇火光閃爍。
西羅特的亡魂！快去擊潰你們的敵人！
唉，希臘！更換的只是主人，境況卻從未改變，
你輝煌的日子已經一去不返，抹不去年代的恥辱。

這個城市由阿拉從加吾爾的手中奪來，
加吾爾再從奧托曼族的手中奪去；
那蘇丹警衛森嚴的樓閣和宮殿，
會迎接暴戾的西方人，那過往的來客，
那作亂的瓦哈比族，既然一度膽敢
從穆罕默德墓前奪去戰利的聖物，
也許將從西方踏著一條血路迂迴而來；
呵，唯有自由的足跡不在這命定的國土降臨，
在無盡苦役的歲月中，只見奴隸們代代相襲。

Hereditary bondsmen! know ye not

Who would be free themselves must strike the blow!

By their right arms the conquest must be wrought!

Will Gaul or Muscovite redress ye? No!

True, they may lay your proud despoilers low,

But not for you will freedom's altars flame.

Shades of the Helots! triumph o'er your foe:

Greece! change thy lords, thy state is still the same;

Thy glorious day is o'er, but not thy years of shame.

The city won for Allah from the Giaour,

The Giaour from Othman's race again may wrest;

And the Serai's impenetrable tower

Receive the fiery Frank, her former guest;

Or Wahab's rebel brood, who dared divest

The Prophet's tomb of all its pious spoil,

May wind their path of blood along the West;

But ne'er will Freedom seek this fated soil,

But slave succeed to slave through years of endless toil.

噢，哭吧，為那些 ╱

I

噢，哭泣吧，為那些在巴比倫河畔哭泣的人們，

他們的聖殿已經傾圮，他們的土地成為一個夢想；

哭泣吧，為猶大那軀殼已經破碎的豎琴，

褻瀆眾神的罪人已住進了他們的神曾經住過之所！

II

啊，以色列那流血的腳將在哪裡洗淨？

啊，錫安山那般美妙的歌何時可以再次聆聽？

猶大的音樂何時能再度奏起，

讓萬民的心重新在那神聖的曲調裡飛騰起舞？

III

你們怎能逃亡而求永遠的安息，

啊，浪跡天涯、心靈疲倦的民族！

野鴿有它的巢，狐狸有它的穴，

人有他的祖國——而以色列卻只有墳墓！

Oh! Weep for Those

I

OH! weep for those that wept by Babel's stream,

Whose shrines are desolate, whose land a dream;

Weep for the harp of Judah's broken shell;

Mourn — where their God that dwelt the godless dwell!

II

And where shall Israel lave her bleeding feet?

And when shall Zion's songs again seem sweet?

And Judah's melody once more rejoice

The hearts that leap'd before its heavenly voice?

III

Tribes of the wandering foot and weary breast,

How shall ye flee away and be at rest!

The wild-dove hath her nest, the fox his cave,

Mankind their country — Israel but the grave!

在約旦河岸邊 ／

阿拉伯人的駱駝迷失在約旦河岸邊，
異教神的信徒們在錫安山頂上祈禱，
太陽神的教士在塞乃峭壁上膜拜——
甚至在那裡——上帝啊，就在那裡，你的雷聲還在沉
睡。

在那裡，方石銘文曾炙烤你的手指！
在那裡，你的影子普照過你的人民！
現在，你的榮耀卻被籠罩在火焰裡：
而你——沒有世人的仰望怎能不死去！

噢，讓你的目光在電閃雷鳴中顯現吧；
讓暴虐者的長矛在他戰慄的手中斬斷！
你的土地還要被暴君們踐踏到什麼時候？
上帝啊，你的廟宇還要冷清到什麼時候？

On Jordan's Banks

On Jordan's banks the Arab's camels stray,
On Sion's hill the False One's votaries pray,
The Baal-adorer bows on Sinai's steep-
Yet there-even there-Oh God! thy thunders sleep:

There-where thy finger scorch'd the tablet stone!
There-where thy shadow to thy people shone!
Thy glory shrouded in its garb of fire:
Thyself-none living see and not expire!

Oh! in the lightning let thy glance appear;
Sweep from his shiver'd hand the oppressor's spear!
How long by tyrants shall thy land be trod?
How long thy temple worshipless, Oh God?

噢！在最嬌豔時被奪去 ／

I

噢！在最嬌豔的時侯被奪去，

笨重的墳墓不會壓在你的身上，

玫瑰花，在那一坏泥土上，

會吐露出早春的新芽，

郊野的柏樹林會鬱鬱地搖曳起伏；

II

多少次，在清澈的泉邊，

「憂傷」使她低垂著頭，

她的思緒充滿各種夢境，

短暫的停留她又輕輕地走了，

可憐的人啊！像是唯恐把死者驚擾。

Oh!Snatch'd Away in Beauty's Bloom

I

Oh! snatch'd away in beauty's bloom,

On thee shall press no ponderous tomb;

But on thy turf shall roses rear

Their leaves, the earliest of the year;

And the wild cypress wave in tender gloom:

II

And oft by yon blue gushing stream

Shall Sorrow lean her drooping head,

And feed deep thought with many a dream,

And lingering pause and lightly tread;

Fond wretch !as if her step disturb'd the dead!

III

走了！我們明知流淚也徒勞，

死者不會理睬，也聽不見我們的悲傷，

這難道就是在教我們

哭得少些？

或不再哀怨？

可你，勸我遺忘，

你的臉色蒼白，淚濕了兩眼。

III

Away !we know that tears are vain,

That death nor heeds nor hears distress:

ill this unteach us to complain?

Or make one mourner weep the less?

And thou — who tell'st me to forget,

Thy looks are wan, thine eyes are wet.

沙魯王最後一戰之歌 ╱

I

勇士和酋長們！如果長矛或利劍
在我率領主的大軍時穿刺我的胸膛，
別理會我的屍體，儘管我是國王，
要把你們的劍插入高斯人的胸膛！

II

還有，無論誰拿了我的盾和弓，
如果沙魯的士兵不敢與敵人對視，
就把我橫放在你腳下的血泊中，
讓我先承當這令他們喪膽的命運。

III

和大家告別了，但永不和你們分離，
哦，我心愛的兒子，我王室的後嗣！
王冠輝煌，王權無邊，
若今天就是死亡之日，讓我們死得偉大！

Warriors and Chiefs

I

Warriors and chiefs! should the shaft or the sword

Pierce me in leading the host of the Lord,

Heed not the corse, though a king's, in your path:

Bury your steel in the bosoms of Gath!

II

Thou who art bearing my buckler and bow,

Should the soldiers of Saul look away from the foe,

Stretch me that moment in blood at thy feet!

Mine be the doom which they dared not to meet.

III

Farewell to others, but never we part,

Heir to my royalty, son of my heart!

Bright is the diadem, boundless the sway,

Or kingly the death, which awaits us to-day!

伯沙撒的幻想 ／

I

巴比倫王端坐在他的寶座上，

大廳擠滿了大臣，

一千盞明亮的燈火

照耀著歡樂的盛宴。

一千盞金杯，

在猶大聖名傳播——

耶和華的器皿裡卻盛著

褻瀆神靈的異教徒的酒漿！

Vision of Belshazzar

I

The King was on his throne,

The satraps throng'd the hall:

A thousand bright lamps shone

O'er that high festival

A thousand cups of gold,

In Judah deem'd divine-

Jehovah's vessels hold

The godless Heathen's wine!

II

就在那一刻，大廳中，
伸出一隻手。
手指在牆上揮舞書寫，
如同在沙灘上寫字：
是一個男人的手指——
啊，一隻獨一無二的手
像一根魔杖
劃出了幾行字跡。

III

國王見了不由一驚，
他的臉色白如蠟；
急忙吩咐停止歡鬧，
他的聲音在顫抖。
「把有學識的人叫來，
讓最賢明的人來解釋，
這破壞皇家歡樂的
是什麼樣的恐怖文字。」

II

In that same hour and hall,

The fingers of a hand

Came forth against the wall,

And wrote as if on sand:

The fingers of a man;-

A solitary hand

Along the letters ran,

And traced them like a wand.

III

The monarch saw, and shook,

And bade no more rejoice;

All bloodless wax'd his look,

And tremulous his voice.

"Let the men of lore appear,

The wisest of the earth,

And expound the words of fear,

Which mar our royal mirth."

IV

迦勒底的預言家雖技藝高超，

但在這裡他們無計可施，

那些可怕的文字仍神祕地

擺在那兒，不為人知。

巴比倫智慧的年長者

滿腹經綸學識淵博；

但是現在他們卻一臉茫然，

不能再被稱為聖者。

V

國中有一位俘虜，

是個異邦的青年，

他聽到國王的旨意，

他來看那文字的真實預言。

周圍的燈火通明，

那預言赫然醒目；

當晚他把它破解，

次日真正地證明了這一點。

IV

Chaldea's seers are good,

But here they have no skill;

And the unknown letters stood

Untold and awful still.

And Babel's men of age

Are wise and deep in lore;

But now they were not sage,

They saw-but knew no more.

V

A captive in the land,

A stranger and a youth,

He heard the king's command,

He saw that writing's truth.

The lamps around were bright,

The prophecy in view;

He read it on that night-

The morrow proved it true.

VI

「伯沙撒墓已掘好，

他的王國已經傾覆，

把他放在天秤一秤

也不過是卑賤的泥土。

屍衣，那是他的皇袍，

墓碑，那是他的華蓋，

米堤亞人闖入他的門前！

波斯人登上了他的寶座！」

VI

"Belshazzar's grave is made,

His kingdom pass'd away,

He, in the balance weigh'd,

Is light and worthless clay;

The shroud his robe of state,

His canopy the stone;

The Mede is at his gate!

The Persian on his throne!"

森納恰瑞伯的滅亡 ╱

I

亞述人來了，像突襲羊群的狼，

他的軍隊閃著紫色和金色光芒，

當夜晚加利的藍色波濤在翻滾，

他們手執長矛的光輝好似海上星宿。

II

日落時，看那大軍揮舞的旗幟

猶如盛夏森林裡的綠葉，

當瑟瑟秋風吹起，

次日清晨，那大軍已枯萎，滿地飄零。

III

因為死神在這狂瀾上蔓延開來，

它飛翔著，對著敵人的臉輕輕吹氣，

那些沉睡的眼睛開始發青，變冷，

他們的心只跳了一下，便再無聲息！

The Destruction of Sennacherib

I

The Assyrian came down like the wolf on the fold,

And his cohorts were gleaming in purple and gold;

And the sheen of their spears was like stars on the sea,

When the blue wave rolls nightly on deep Galilee.

II

Like the leaves of the forest when Summer is green,

That host with their banners at sunset were seen:

Like the leaves of the forest when Autumn hath blown,

That host on the morrow lay wither'd and strown.

III

For the Angel of Death spread his wings on the blast,

And breathed in the face of the foe as he passed;

And the eye of the sleepers wax'd deadly and chill,

And their hearts but once heaved, and for ever grew still!

IV

戰馬也倒下了，大張著鼻孔，

但裡面不再流淌著驕傲和自豪的氣息；

馬喘息著吐出的白沫還留在草地上，

冰冷得好像撞擊在岩石上的波浪。

V

騎馬的壯士也躺著，面色蒼白、扭曲，

露珠凝結在他的眉頭，鎧甲上長滿了鏽；

帳篷裡一片死寂，只剩下旗幟，

沒有人再舉起槍，也無人吹軍號。

VI

而亞述的寡婦們在大聲哭喊，

巴力廟宇中的神像已被打碎；

這異教徒的武力未及交鋒，

上帝只一瞥，便像雪似的消融了。

IV

And there lay the steed with his nostril all wide,

But through it there rolled not the breath of his pride;

And the foam of his gasping lay white on the turf,

And cold as the spray of the rock-beating surf.

V

And there lay the rider distorted and pale,

With the dew on his brow, and the rust on his mail;

And the tents were all silent, the banners alone,

The lances unlifted, the trumpet unblown.

VI

And the widows of Ashur are loud in their wail,

And the idols are broke in the temple of Baal;

And the might of the Gentile, unsmote by the sword,

Hath melted like snow in the glance of the Lord!

我願做無憂無慮的孩童 ╱

I

我願做個無憂無慮的孩童，

棲身於廣闊高原的洞穴：

在朦朧的原野裡遊蕩，

在深藍色的波浪上騰躍。

撒克遜浮華的繁文縟節，

正與我自由的靈魂相背離：

坡道崎嶇的山地令我眷戀，

怒濤澎湃的巨石讓我神往。

I Would I were a Careless Child

I

I would I were a careless child,

Still dwelling in my Highland cave,

Or roaming through the dusky wild,

Or bounding o'er the dark blue wave;

The cumbrous pomp of Saxon pride,

Accords not with the freeborn soul,

Which loves the mountain's craggy side,

And seeks the rocks where billows roll.

II

命運啊，請收回富饒的田地，

收回這響亮的尊貴稱號！

我厭惡看人們低三下四，

我憎恨奴僕的阿諛左右，

讓我回到我所摯愛的地方，

聽岩石和大海隨聲附和的呼嘯：

那是我從小就熟悉的風光，

只求讓我再次看到。

III

年少的我已經察覺到。

這個世界不屬於我。

啊！幽冥的黑暗為何要掩蓋

世人向塵寰的辭別？

夢境中的輝煌，我也曾經擁有，

那是極樂之鄉神奇的幻覺；

現實！你為何用這可恨的明亮，

引領我來到這樣一個俗世。

II

Fortune! take back these cultured lands,

Take back this name of splendid sound!

I hate the touch of servile hands,

I hate the slaves that cringe around.

Place me among the rocks I love,

Which sound to Ocean's wildest roar;

I ask but this-again to rove

Through scenes my youth hath known before.

III

Few are my years, and yet I feel

The world was ne'er design'd for me:

Ah! why do dark'ning shades conceal

The hour when man must cease to be?

Once I beheld a splendid dream,

A visionary scene of bliss:

Truth!— wherefore did thy hated beam

Awake me to a world like this?

IV

愛情離我遠去，

友誼也早已終了；

這樣的心靈怎能不孤寂，

當原有的希望都已破滅。

雖有歡謔的友伴舉杯相邀，

惡劣情懷只能在瞬間遠逃；

縱飲可使癡狂的靈魂振奮，

可心兒啊，依然孤獨傷悲。

V

聽他們高談闊論多無聊，

這群人與我無關，

可門第、權勢、財富或機遇，

卻使我們筵前相見。

請還我幾個忠實的朋友！

請還我原有的青春和愛情！

逃離那夜半喧囂的應酬，

他們的歡樂只不過徒有虛名。

IV

I loved-but those I loved are gone;

Had friends-my early friends are fled:

How cheerless feels the heart alone,

When all its former hopes are dead!

Though gay companions, o'er the bowl

Dispel awhile the sense of ill;

Though Pleasure stirs the maddening soul,

The heart, the heart, is lonely still.

V

How dull! to hear the voice of those

Whom rank or chance, whom wealth or power,

Have made, though neither friends nor foes,

Associates of the festive hour.

Give me again a faithful few,

In years and feelings still the same,

And I will fly the midnight crew,

Where boist'rous joy is but a name.

VI

美麗的人啊，難道你就是

我的希望、慰藉和我的一切？

連你的微笑也失了魅力，

我的心怎能不充滿寒意！

世俗是那麼富麗和淒苦，

我願從此告別，毫不惋惜。

恬靜令我怡然知足——

美德與它似曾相識。

VII

遁離這熙熙攘攘的世界——

不是厭惡，只想逃避。

我要尋覓幽靜的山谷，

讓陰沉的胸懷與冥色相繞。

請給我一雙翅膀：

像飛回巢中的斑鳩，

我也要展翅淩空，

飄然遠行，永久安寧！

VI

And woman, lovely woman! thou,

My hope, my comforter, my all!

How cold must be my bosom now,

When e'en thy smiles begin to pall!

Without a sigh would I resign,

This busy scene of splendid woe,

To make that calm contentment mine,

Which virtue knows, or seems to know.

VII

Fain would I fly the haunts of men-

I seek to shun, not hate mankind;

My breast requires the sullen glen,

Whose gloom may suit a darken'd mind.

Oh! that to me the wings were given,

Which bear the turtle to her nest!

Then would I cleave the vault of Heaven,

To flee away, and be at rest

最大的悲傷 ╱

什麼是等待年老的最大悲傷？

是什麼把皺紋深深烙進額頭？

是看著每個親人從生命冊上被刪去，

獨自苟活於人間，像我現在這樣。

啊，讓我在懲罰者面前低頭，

為被分離的心、為破碎的希望默哀，

無用的歲月啊，流逝吧！你盡管無憂無慮，

因為歲月已奪走了我一切所愛，

晚年的病痛也腐蝕了我早年的歡樂。

The Worst of Woes

What is the worst of woes that wait on age?

What stamps the wrinkle deeper on the brow?

To view each loved one blotted from life's page,

And be alone on earth, as I am now.

Before the chastener humbly let me bow,

O'er hearts divided and o'er hopes destroyed:

Roll on, vain days! full reckless may ye flow,

Since Time hath reft whate'er my soul enjoyed,

And with the ills of eld mine earlier years alloyed.

義大利的黃昏／

月亮升起來了，但還不是夜晚，

落日和月亮平分天穹，

霞光的海洋沿著藍色弗留利群山的高巔

洶湧奔流，

天空無雲，卻好像交織著各種顏色，

融匯成西方的一彎巨大彩虹，

白晝連接了逝去的永恆；

而對面，月中的山峰

浮游於蔚藍的空氣——神聖的海島！

At Dusk in Italy

The moon is up, and yet it is not night;

Sunset divides the sky with her; a sea

Of glory streams along the Alpine height

Of blue Friuli's mountains; Heaven is free

From clouds, but of all colours seems to be,-

Melted to one vast Iris of the West, -

Where the Day joins the past Eternity,

While, on the other hand, meek Dian's crest

Floats through the azure air - an island of the blest!

只有一顆孤星伴著戴安娜，和她一起守護著

這半壁恬靜的天空，但在那邊

日光之海仍舊燦爛，它的波濤

仍舊在遙遠的瑞申山頂上翻滾流轉；

白晝和黑夜在互相爭奪，直到大自然

恢復它原來的秩序：幽暗的布倫泰河

輕柔地流淌著，晝夜給它注入了

初開放玫瑰花的芬芳，

這紫色順水而流，就像是在鏡面上閃爍，

河面上充滿了從遙遠的天庭

降臨的面容；

水面上的各種色彩

從斑斕落日到升起的明星，

都將它們的奇光異彩散發、融合：

啊，現在變色了；冉冉的陰影飄過，

把它的帷幕掛上山巒；即將告別的白天

仿佛是瀕臨死亡的、不斷喘息的海豚，

每一陣劇痛都使它的顏色改變，

越來越美妙；終於——結束了——一切沒入了灰色。

A single star is at her side, and reigns

With her o'er half the lovely heaven; but still

Yon sunny sea heaves brightly, and remains

Roll'd o'er the peak of the far Rhtian hill,

As day and night contending were, until

Nature reclaim'd her order: — gently flows

The deep-dyed Brenta, where their hues instil

The odorous purple of a new-born rose,

Which streams upon her stream, and glass'd within it glows,

Fill'd with the face of heaven, which, from afar,

Comes down upon the waters; all its hues,

From the rich sunset to the rising star,

Their magical variety diffuse:

And now they change; a paler shadow strews

Its mantle o'er the mountains; parting day

Dies like the dolphin, whom each pang imbues

With a new colour as it gasps away-

The last still loveliest, -till, 'tis gone, and all is gray.

荒墟 ╱

啊，時間啊！你把逝去的一切美化了，
你把荒墟裝飾了，唯有你可以撫慰
和醫治我們受傷的心靈；
時間啊！你可以糾正我們錯誤的判斷，
你考驗真理，愛——是唯一的哲人，
其他都是詭辯家，因為只有你
雖不輕易言語且說話緩慢，卻言必中肯。

The Wreck

Oh Time! the beautifier of the dead,

Adorner of the ruin, comforter

And only healer when the heart hath bled;

Time! the corrector where our judgments err,

The test of truth, love, -sole philosopher,

For all beside are sophists - from thy thrift,

Which never loses though it doth defer-

時間啊，你也是個報復者！我舉起

我的手、眼睛和心，向你索要一件禮物：

在這荒墟中，請建立

一座廟宇和神壇，更為冷清、莊嚴，

在你貴重的祭品中，有我

歲月的荒墟，儘管短暫，卻悲歡盡含。

啊，如果你曾見我洋洋得意，

不要理睬；但如果我平靜地接受

好運，而在那制伏不了我的狠毒面前

保持高傲，請不要讓我的靈魂

徒然地負上這塊鐵──難道他們不悔恨？

Time, the avenger! unto thee I lift

My hands, and eyes, and heart, and crave of thee a gift:

Amidst this wreck, where thou hast made a shrine

And temple more divinely desolate,

Among thy mightier offerings here are mine,

Ruins of years, though few, yet full of fate:

If thou hast ever seen me too elate,

Hear me not; but if calmly I have borne

Good, and reserved my pride against the hate

Which shall not whelm me, let me not have worn

This iron in my soul in vain-shall they not mourn?

東方 ╱

你可知道有個地方，柏樹和桃金娘

是那片土地上發生的所有事情的見證？

在那裡，禿鷲的憤怒和海龜的愛情

一會兒化為哀傷，一會兒狂橫暴行！

你知道那生長雪松和藤蔓的地方，

鮮花永遠盛開，陽光永遠明媚；

芬芳壓低了西風輕盈的翅膀，

在玫瑰盛開的園中逐漸偃息。

在那，香櫞和橄欖是最好的水果，

夜鶯終年不停地歌唱；

那兒的土地和天空儘管色彩各異，

卻爭奇鬥艷，

而海洋的紫那麼深，那麼濃厚。

The Clime of The East

Know ye the land where the cypress and myrtle

Are emblems of deeds that are done in their clime?

Where the rage of the vulture, the love of the turtle,

Now melt into sorrow, now madden to crime!

Know ye the land of the cedar and vine,

Where the flowers ever blossom, the beams ever shine;

Where the light wings of zephyr, oppress'd with perfume,

Wax faint o'er the gardens of Gúl in her bloom;

Where the citron and olive are fairest of fruit,

And the voice of the nightingale never is mute:

Where the tints of the earth, and the hues of the sky,

In colour though varied, in beauty may vie,

And the purple of ocean is deepest in dye;

少女好像她們摘下的玫瑰一樣甜美溫柔，

挽救人類的精神，是神聖的？

噢，那裡是東方，太陽升起的地方——

他能否對他子女的行為微笑、稱讚？

啊，猶如愛人告別的聲音一樣熾熱，

那是他們的愛心，和他們要講的故事。

Where the virgins are soft as the roses they twine,

And all, save the spirit of man, is divine?

'Tis the clime of the East; 't is the land of the Sun-

Can he smile on such deeds as his children have done?

Oh ! wild as the accents of lovers farewell

Ar the hearts which they bear, and the tales which they tell.

海盜生涯 ╱

在湛藍的海上，海水在歡快地飛濺，
我們的心如此自由，我們的思緒遼遠無邊，
廣袤啊，盡長風吹拂之地、凡海波翻捲之處，
量一量我們的版圖，看一看我們的家鄉！
這全是我們的帝國，它的權力橫掃一切——
我們的旗幟就是王笏，所遇莫有不從。
我們粗獷的生涯，在風暴動盪中
從勞作到休息，什麼樣的日子都有樂趣。
噢，誰能體會？絕不是你，嬌養的奴僕！
你的靈魂對著起伏波浪就會退縮；
更不是你安樂荒淫和虛榮的主人！
睡眠不能撫慰你，歡樂也難令你開心。
誰知那樂趣，除非他的心受過折磨，
又在廣闊的海洋上驕傲地翱翔過。
那狂喜的感覺、那脈搏暢快的歡跳，
可不只有絕境求生的遊蕩者才能體會。

The Corsair

O'er the glad waters of the dark blue sea,

Our thoughts as boundless, and our soul's as free

Far as the breeze can bear, the billows foam,

Survey our empire, and behold our home!

These are our realms, no limits to their sway-

Our flag the sceptre all who meet obey.

Ours the wild life in tumult still to range

From toil to rest, and joy in every change.

Oh, who can tell? not thou, luxurious slave!

Whose soul would sicken o'er the heaving wave;

Not thou, vain lord of wantonness and ease!

whom slumber soothes not - pleasure cannot please-

Oh, who can tell, save he whose heart hath tried,

And danced in triumph o'er the waters wide,

The exulting sense - the pulse's maddening play,

That thrills the wanderer of that trackless way?

是這快樂使我們去追尋那迎頭的鬥爭，
是這快樂把看似危險的事物變為歡笑；
凡是懦夫躲避的，我們必去熱烈尋追，
那使衰弱的人暈厥的，我們反而感到——
感覺在我們博大胸懷的最深處，
希望在蘇醒，精靈在翱翔。

我們不畏死亡，我們寧願與敵人共死一處，
雖然，沒能壽終正寢讓人略覺遺憾。
來吧，隨它高興——我們攫取了生中之生，
如果倒下——誰在乎是死於刀劍還是疾病？
讓那些爬行的人去跟「衰老」長久纏綿，
讓他們黏在自己的臥榻上，苦度年歲；
讓他們搖著麻痹的頭顱，艱難地喘息，
我們不要病床，寧可躺在清新的綠草上。
當他一喘一喘地咳出他的靈魂，
我們只在一剎那的疼痛中超脫。

That for itself can woo the approaching fight,

And turn what some deem danger to delight;

That seeks what cravens shun with more than zeal,

And where the feebler faint can only feel-

Feel-to the rising bosom's inmost core,

Its hope awaken and Its spirit soar?

No dread of death if with us die our foes-

Save that it seems even duller than repose:

Come when it will-we snatch the life of life-

When lost-what recks it but disease or strife?

Let him who crawls enamour'd of decay,

Cling to his couch, and sicken years away:

Heave his thick breath, and shake his palsied head;

Ours-the fresh turf; and not the feverish bed.

While gasp by gasp he falters forth his soul,

Ours with one pang-one bound-escapes control.

讓他們的屍首去誇耀它的陋穴和骨灰甕，

憎恨他一生的人會為他的墓座鑲金；

我們的葬禮將伴著珍貴的真情之淚

——當海波覆蓋和收斂我們的軀體。

對於我們，即便是歡宴也會帶來深刻的痛惜，

在紅色酒杯中旋起我們的記憶；

啊，危險的日子最終化作簡短的墓誌銘，

當勝利的夥伴們平分寶藏，卻潛然淚下，

當回憶黯淡了每人的前額，

現在，那倒下的勇士得以欣然長辭。

His corse may boast its urn and narrow cave,

And they who loath'd his life may gild his grave:

Ours are the tears, though few, sincerely shed,

When Ocean shrouds and sepulchres our dead.

For us, even banquets fond regret supply

In the red cup that crowns our memory;

And the brief epitaph in danger's day,

When those who win at length divide the prey,

And cry, remembrance saddening o'er each brow,

How had the brave who fell exulted now!

詩創作 ╱

我不僅惹得這個世界喧囂，

還激怒了他人——那些教士們

在我頭上讓天雷轟隆劈下，

再虔誠地將我侮辱一番。

可是我還是忍不住每星期亂寫一篇，

老讀者已厭煩，卻沒有新作出現。

年少時，是因為滿腹理想寫作，

而現在則覺得它日漸乏味而寫。

但是「何必發表呢？」——如果讓人厭倦，

就不可能獲得名或利的報酬。

那我要問——你們為什麼要玩牌，

飲酒或讀書？為了讓時間不那麼難熬。

而我的消遣就是要回顧一下

我的所見所思，無論是難過還是歡樂。

我把我寫的扔進時間的長河裡，

任它沉浮——至少我曾有過夢。

Writing

I have brought this world about my ears, and eke

The other; that's to say, the clergy, who

Upon my head have bid their thunders break

In pious libels by no means a few.

And yet I can't help scribbling once a week,

Tiring old readers, nor discovering new.

In youth I wrote because my mind was full,

And now because I feel it growing dull.

But "why then publish?"-There are no rewards

Of fame or profit when the world grows weary.

I ask in turn-Why do you play at cards?

Why drink? Why read-To make some hour less dreary.

It occupies me to turn back regards

On what I've seen or ponder'd, sad or cheery;

And what I write I cast upon the stream,

To swim or sink-I have had at least my dream.

地主們 ／

哦，鄉土！怎樣的語言或筆墨，

才可以悲歎地描述她那沒有鄉情的鄉紳？

最不願使戰爭的叫囂停止的是他們，

第一個認為和平是場瘟疫的是他們。

這些鄉間的愛國人士緣何而生？

難道是為了打獵、選舉和使穀價上升？

但穀價像世俗的一切一樣必然會下跌；

多數的國王、征服者和市場，

難道你們必須要隨著每一束穀穗淪落？

為什麼你們要為龐納派特王朝的統治而煩惱？

Tillers

Alas, the country !How shall tongue or pen

Bewail her now uncountry gentlemen?

The last to bid the cry of warfare cease,

The first to make a malady of peace.

For what were all these country patriots born?

To hunt, and vote, and raise the price of corn?

But corn, like every mortal thing, must fall,

Kings, conquerors, and markets most of all.

And must ye fall with every ear of grain?

Why would you trouble Buonaparte's reign?

他是你們的崔普托雷瑪斯，他的罪惡

只是摧毀了王國，卻仍舊保持了你們的價格；

他增強了每位領主的滿足欲

——那偉大的農業淘金術、高價的租金。

為什麼他們的暴君臣服於韃靼人，

並且小麥的價格貶到如此令人失望的地步？

為什麼你們把他鎖在孤獨的小島？

那傢伙稱王時有很大的價值。

的確，鮮血和財富都曾無止境地溢出，

那又怎樣？讓高盧擔當這罪惡；

麵包漲價了，農民仍以他的方式付款，

約定的日子，田地被報以酬勞。

而現在，那醇香的「付酬酒」哪裡去了？

何處去尋那從不肯拖欠的佃戶？

何處去尋那從不荒閑的田莊？

何處去尋那沼澤地的拓荒和耕種？

何處去尋那租約到期急切的等待？

He was your great Triptolemus; his vices

Destroy'd but realms, and still maintain'd your prices;

He amplified to every lord's content

The grand agrarian alchymy, high rent.

Why did they tyrant stumble on the Tartars,

And lower wheat to such desponding quarters?

Why did you chain him on yon isle so lone?

The man was worth much more upon this throne.

True, blood and treasure boundlessly were spilt,

But what of that? the Gaul may bear the guilt;

But bread was high, the farmer paid his way,

And acres told upon the appointed day.

But where is now the goodly audit ale?

The purse-proud tenant, never known to fail?

The farm which never yet was left on hand?

The marsh reclaim'd to must improving land?

The impatient hope of the expiring lease?

還有那加倍的租金？哦，好一個罪惡的和平！

枉然地用獎金鼓勵農民增產，

下議院也白白通過愛國議案；

地主們從此處到彼處為自己的利益呻吟，

怕的是「豐衣足食」也降臨到窮人身上。

高些，再高些，地租！高舉你的意見，

否則內閣就要喪失它的選票，

而愛國的情緒，脆弱的美麗，

她的麵包就要跌到市面的價格。

The doubling rental? What an evil's peace !

In vain the prize excites the ploughman's skill,

In vain the commons pass their patriot bill;

The landed interest- (you may understand

The phrase much better leaving out the land)-

The land self-interest groans from shore to shore,

For fear that plenty should attain the poor.

Up, up again, ye rents !exalt your notes,

Or else the ministry will lose their votes,

And patriotism, so delicately nice,

Her loaves will lower to the market price;

唉！麵包和魚價錢曾經如此之高，

現在完了——他們的烤爐關了門，他們的海洋正乾涸；

百萬家財散盡後一無所有，

除了增長的中庸和滿足。

不是這樣的，請等一等，

好運的公平之甕這才靜靜地送來；

讓他們的美德充當自己的報酬。

現在，讓另一批夥伴去自作自受，

請看這些可恥的辛辛芮塔斯蜂群，

戰爭的播種者、田莊的獨裁者，

他們的鋤頭是雇工手中的鋒劍，

異國所流的血肥沃了他們的田地；

守著自己的穀倉，這些塞賓的地主們

把同胞送去作戰——為什麼？為了租金！

For ah ! "the loaves and fishes," once so high,

Are gone - their oven closed, their ocean dry,

And nought remains of all the millions spent,

Excepting to grow moderate and content.

They who are not so, had their turn - and turn

About still flows from Fortune's equal urn;

Now let their virtue be its own reward,

And share the blessings which themselves prepared.

See these inglorious Cincinnati swarm,

Farmers of war, dictators of the farm;

Their ploughshare was the sword in hireling hands,

Their fields manured by gore of other lands;

Safe in their barns, these Sabine tillers sent

Their brethen out to battle - why? for rent !

一年又一年，他們全體投票贊成

用血、汗和眼淚敲詐出數以百萬的財富。

為什麼？為了租金！

他們呼喊，他們宴飲，他們宣誓一定

要為英國而死——為什麼仍活著呢？為了租金！

和平已經讓這些高度市場化的愛國人士

普遍不滿：因為，戰爭曾經是租金！

他們對祖國的熱愛，和隨便使用的百萬家財，

怎樣去協調？只有解決地租的爭端！

難道他們不用償還財富的貸款？

不，打倒一切，只要地租無邊際地上升！

他們的善惡、健康、財富、失望，

及生命、終點、目的、宗教，就是——租金、租金、

租金！

Year after year they voted cent per cent.

Blood, sweat, and tear-wrung millions - why? for rent !

They roar'd, they dined, they drank, they swore they meant

To die for England - why then live? - for rent !

The peace has made one general malcontent

Of these high-market patriots; war was rent !

Their love of country, millions all misspent,

How reconcile? by reconciling rent !

And will they not repay the treasures lent?

No; down with everything, and up with rent !

Their good, ill, health, wealth, joy, or discontent,

Being, end, aim, religion - rent, rent, rent !

我不是不愛人類，但我更愛自然／

哦，但願這片沙漠是我的居所，

用一種美麗的心靈作我的牧師，

借此或許我可以完全忘記人類，

而且不恨任何人，只愛她一個！

偉大的自然元素啊！在你激勵的

點醒中，我感覺到了自己的昂揚鬥志，

你能不能賦予我這樣一個生命？

難道我錯了：認為她們的寓居並不少？

雖然我們很少有和她們款款細語的幸運之籤。

I Love Not Man the Less, But Nature More

Oh! that the desert were my dwelling-place,

With one fair spirit for my minster,

That I might all forget the human race,

And, hating no one, love but only her!

Ye Elements!- in whose ennobling stir

I feel myself exalted - Can ye not

Accord me such a being? Do I err

In deeming such inhabit many a spot?

Though with them to converse can rarely be our lot.

在那荒無人跡的森林有一種樂趣，

在那寂寥的海岸邊有一種歡欣，

這裡是一個無人侵擾的社會，

在那海的深處，海嘯伴著濤聲嗚咽。

我不是不愛人類，但我更愛自然，

從這些和自然的邂逅，我偷偷從我過去的一切中逃離，

和那茫茫廣宇融成一體，我的心緒

絕非言語所能表達——但也無法隱匿！

翻騰吧，你這幽深而暗藍的海洋，

一萬艘軍艦徒勞地在你的身上掠過；

人類給陸地留下許多荒墟，他的統治

卻到陸地的邊沿為止；那莽原澤國

浮著的殘骸都是你的傑作，還不曾留下

人類蹂躪的一絲陰影，除了他渺小的自己，

恰似一滴雨珠，一剎那間向海上墜落，

汩汩地冒泡、呻吟，沉沒在你深深的懷抱，

沒有墓園，沒有教堂的鐘聲，

不見棺材，也沒有人知道。

There is a pleasure in the pathless woods,

There is a rapture on the lonely shore,

There is society, where none intrudes,

By the deep sea, and music in its roar:

I love not man the less, but nature more,

From these our interviews, in which I steal

From all I may be, or have been before,

To mingle with the universe, and feel

What I can ne'er express, yet cannot all conceal.

Roll on, thou deep and dark blue ocean - roll!

Ten thousand fleets sweep over thee in vain;

Man marks the earth with ruin - his control

Stops with the shore; - upon the watery plain

The wrecks are all thy deed, nor doth remain

A shadow of man's ravage, save his own,

When for a moment, like a drop of rain,

He sinks into thy depths with bubbling groan,

Without a grave, unknelled, uncoffined, and unknown.

他的足跡不在你的道路、你的領地之上

那不是他的戰利品，——你翻騰起來

把他從身上搖落——你蔑視

他控制的邪惡力量，因為它給大地只帶來災難；

你把他從你的胸膛拋上天空，

你把他遠逐，他在你嬉戲的浪花上顫抖；

他向他的上帝哀號，你把他送往

他渺小希望所寄託的臨近港口和海灣，

又將他扔回陸地把他安放在那兒。

那像雷霆一樣轟擊石築城牆的

海軍的重炮，它的威力使天下顫抖，

君王在他們的首府裡也戰慄，

還有那橡木造的龐然大物，它巨大的船架

曾使它泥制的造物主虛榮地

自封為海洋的主人，戰爭勝負的主人。

但這一切不過是你的玩具——像雪片一樣，

它們都溶進你波濤的泡沫裡，你能損毀

阿馬達的光榮，或是特拉法爾加的劫掠。

His steps are not upon thy paths, - thy fields

Are not a spoil for him, - thou dost arise

And shake him from thee; the vile strength he wields

For earth's destruction thou dost all despise,

Spurning him from thy bosom to the skies,

And send'st him, shivering in thy playful spray

And howling to his Gods, where haply lies

His petty hope in some near port or bay,

And dash him again to earth: - there let him lay.

The armaments which thunder - strike the walls

Of rock-built cities, bidding nations quake,

And monarchs tremble in their capitals,

The oak leviathans, whose huge ribs make

Their clay creator the vain title take

Of lord of thee, and arbiter of war;

These are thy toys, and, as the snowy flake,

They melt into thy yeast of waves, which mar

Alike the Armada's pride, or spoils of Trafalgar.

你的岸上帝國已物是人非，只有你不會改變——

亞述、希臘、羅馬、迦太基，它們又如何？

當他們自由之時你的波濤淘去了它們的強權，

之後多少世的暴君：他們的海岸聽從著

異邦人、奴隸或者野蠻人；他們的衰亡

使王國乾涸變為沙漠；但你卻不同——

你那激烈的波濤不曾改變。

在你碧藍的額際，時間沒有描上一道皺紋：

從開天闢地到現在，你一直是這樣滔滔不絕。

啊，你這光輝的明鏡！上帝把自己的丰姿

在暴風雨中映照出來；無論是平靜

還是震動，是微風還是狂風，

無論是在冰凍的極地，還是在炎熱的氣候，

幽暗、起伏。你無涯、無盡而莊嚴，

你永恆的形象，是無形的王座，

甚至深海裡的珍奇異獸

也是由你的淤泥而生，每片土地

都服從於你；你一如既往，深不見底、可怕而孤獨。

Thy shores are empires, changed in all save thee —

Assyria, Greece, Rome, Carthage, what are they?

Thy waters washed them power while they were free,

And many a tyrant since: their shores obey

The stranger, slave, or savage; their decay

Has dried up realms to deserts: — not so thou,

Unchangeable save to thy wild waves' play —

Time writes no wrinkle on thine azure brow —

Such as creation's dawn beheld, thou rollest now.

Thou glorious mirror, where the Almighty's form

Glasses itself in tempests; in all time,

Calm or convulsed — in breeze, or gale, or storm,

Icing the pole, or in the torrid clime,

Dark--heaving; — boundless, endless, and sublime —

The image of eternity — the throne

Of the Invisible; even from out thy slime

The monsters of the deep are made; each zone

Obeys thee; thou goest forth, dread, fathomless, alone.

可是我一直愛著你，大海！

青春運動的快樂就是被承載在你的胸膛上，

像你的水泡，往前飄浮：從兒時起

我總想與你的巨浪為伴。對於我，

衝擊海浪是一種快樂；而淡化的海

使它們顯得可怕——那也是一種愉快的恐懼，

因為我就像是你的孩子，

因為我信任你遠遠近近、起起浮浮的波濤，

因為我曾用手撫摸著你的鬃毛——猶如現在這樣。

And I have loved thee, ocean! and my joy

of youthful sports was on thy breast to be

borne, like thy bubbles, onward: from a boy

I wanton'd with thy breakers — they to me

Were a delight; and if the freshening sea

Made them a terror — t'was a pleasing fear,

For I was as it were a child of thee,

And trusted to thy billows far and near,

And laid my hand upon thy mane — as I do here.

喬治・戈登・拜倫（George Gordon Byron，1788—1824），英國著名詩人、作家，引領風騷的浪漫主義文學泰斗。

他出生於倫敦一個沒落的貴族家庭，天生即為跛足，母親性格喜怒無常，這成為他內心敏感的要因之一。3 歲時父親過世，10 歲繼承了家族的男爵爵位，人稱「拜倫勳爵」。獲得爵位後，與母親搬至諾丁漢郡生活，在這裡，他看見無數工人為生活勞苦、承受不公不義之事，也因此成為他日後致力於民主運動的種子。

拜倫曾在哈羅公校和劍橋大學讀書，深受啟蒙主義的薰陶，也在此開始學習寫作，利用寫作道出對社會的批判與對貴族的不滿。成年後，正逢歐洲各國民主、民族運動，拜倫心中反對專制、支持民主的先進思想，使他開始參與英國的工人運動，成為 19 世紀初歐洲革命運動中爭取民主自由和民族解放的一名戰士。

拜倫一生為民主、自由、民族解放的理想而奮鬥，也致力於寫作，從學生時期便開始創作詩歌。他的作品具有重大的歷史進步意義和藝術價值，他未完成的長篇詩體小說《唐璜》，便是一部氣勢宏偉、意境開闊、見解高超且卓越的敘事長詩，在英國當地乃至於歐洲文學史上都是罕見的作品。

拜倫熱愛自由，除了支持英國的民主改革外，他也十分同情希臘的獨立運動。1823 年，拜倫放下手邊正在創作的詩歌，號召了一支義勇軍，支援希臘對抗鄂圖曼帝國的獨立戰爭，

卻因為長年勞苦加上在戰區未得到即時的醫療救助，不幸在1824 年亡於希臘。其逝世使得希臘國民哀慟不已，為他舉行國喪，並全國致哀 21 天。

　　既是貴族、又身為革命者的拜倫，寫出的詩歌也把這種深入其生活、思想的矛盾寫入了他的作品當中，因此也被眾人稱為「在最好的作品中不但是個偉大的詩人，而且是世界上總會需要的一種詩人」。

關於作品 ─────────────────────

　　這位多產的詩人，在 1833 年由後人彙總所出的《拜倫詩集》便有 17 卷之多，其中便包括《恰爾德‧哈洛爾德遊記》、《異教徒》、《普羅米修斯》、《錫雍的囚徒》、《曼佛雷特》、《該隱》、《唐璜》等詩。而本書精選了拜倫眾多詩篇當中的代表作，如《當初我倆分別》、《漫步在美的光影》、《我看過你哭》……每一首都是璀璨的經典。

　　拜倫的詩歌諷刺性極強，有著強烈的主觀抒情性和鮮明的政治傾向，其詩的美學核心為「詩的本身即是熱情」，濃郁的感情基調、主角非凡的品質、誇張的感情、異國情調、馳騁的想像力，以及強而有力的浪漫主義都是其作品的魅力表現。

　　本書精選浪漫主義文學泰斗拜倫的最經典篇章。詩人以極高的天賦和對美好生活的執著所創作出的詩歌，將「美」以文字形式展現給世人，從詩中便能看出他對自由的強烈嚮往和熱愛。

1788	0	1月22日出生於英國倫敦。原名為喬治‧戈登‧拜倫，其父母皆出身於沒落貴族家庭。拜倫出生時其中一腳即不良於行，這成為他日後心理敏感的原因之一。
1791	3	父親逝世，拜倫自此跟母親相依為命。
1798	10	拜倫繼承了其伯祖父的世襲爵位和產業，成為拜倫家族的第六代男爵。他和母親移居至諾丁漢郡的世襲領地生活。諾丁漢是當時英國的工業重地，拜倫在這裡成長的同時也知曉了工人所生活的苦難與面臨剝削、壓迫的困境，這帶給他極大的影響。
1801	13	為了使拜倫能夠更好地配上公爵的稱號，家族將其轉進位於倫敦的哈羅公校。
1805	17	拜倫中學畢業，進入劍橋大學，主修文學和歷史。他不常聽課，參與多項娛樂活動，射擊、拳擊、游泳等，看似不學無術的他卻廣泛閱讀歐洲各國文學、哲學以及歷史著作，對啟蒙思想家的著作特別有興趣，研讀了幾乎所有的伏爾泰和盧梭作品，之後也開始創作自己的詩歌。
1807	19	出版了處女作《懶散的時刻》，拜倫透過詩集表達對現實生活的不滿和對貴族生活的厭倦和鄙視，後來此詩集在社會上受到不少攻擊和奚落。面對這些謾罵，拜倫寫出長詩《英國詩人

和蘇格蘭評論家》回擊，意外地揭開了積極浪漫主義與消極浪漫主義的戰爭，這首長詩也使得拜倫在英國詩歌文壇中初露鋒芒。

| 1809 | 21 | 劍橋大學畢業，拜倫因世襲的爵位，在上議院獲得了議員資格。雖然他出席議院和發言的次數不多，但都明確表示了自己自由主義的進步立場。 |

6 月，拜倫開始在地中海國家進行 期兩年的旅行，先後前往葡萄牙、西班牙、馬爾他島、阿爾巴尼亞、希臘和土耳其等地。

| 1811 | 23 | 7 月時，拜倫結束旅行，回到了英國。拜倫的這次旅遊擴展了他的政治視野，也豐富了他的寫作素材，成為他日後寫下《恰爾德・哈洛爾德遊記》的主要背景。 |

| 1812 | 24 | 發表長詩《恰爾德・哈洛爾德遊記》，這使他一夜成名。 |

當時英國國內因民間對抗工業革命呼聲過高，盧德運動四起。2 月時，拜倫為了英國工人權益而辯護，卻不受議會重視，氣急敗壞的拜倫寫下諷刺詩《反對破壞機器法案》。

4 月，拜倫在國會發表演說，支持愛爾蘭獨立，同時發表《給一位哭泣的貴婦人》。

1813	25	發表《異教徒》、《阿比道斯的新娘》等詩。
1814	26	前後發表了《溫莎的詩藝》、《海盜》、《萊拉》等詩歌。
1815	27	與安妮·伊莎貝拉·米爾班克結婚，後育有一女。
1816	28	拜倫發表了《柯林斯的圍攻》、《巴里西納》和《路德分子歌》，這些詩歌被總稱《東方敘事詩》，並塑造出文學史上「拜倫式英雄」的佳話。雖然詩歌為拜倫贏得了巨大的聲譽，但由於其思想和英國政壇截然相反，他受盡政客和上流社會的批評與攻擊。

4月，與妻子安妮·伊莎貝拉·米爾班克離婚，這件事也成為被攻擊的主要目標。因為失敗婚姻、惡意散布的醜聞與債務問題，拜倫離開故土，到比利時參與滑鐵盧戰役。

戰後拜倫去了瑞士，在這認識了詩人珀西·比希·雪萊，兩人成為好友，雪萊的詩歌精神也影響了拜倫。在此期間，拜倫認識了雪萊妻子的妹妹克萊爾·克萊爾蒙特，和她生有一女，但不久即夭折。

因多方遊歷，見到無數歐洲人民的苦難與戰場，拜倫在瑞士日內瓦創作出《普羅米修斯》、《錫雍的囚徒》和《恰爾德·哈洛爾德遊記》第三章，以及悲觀主義詩歌《曼佛雷特》。

		1816 下半年，拜倫前往義大利，投入燒炭黨人的運動中，成為地方組織的領袖。
1819	30	在義大利滯留期間，與當地貴族的妻子特蕾莎·古奇奧利發生婚外情。這段時間拜倫創作了《恰爾德·哈洛爾德遊記》第四章、《馬力諾·法里埃羅》、《該隱》、《審判的幻景》、《青銅世紀》和《唐璜》，這時期他的創作達到了最高峰。
1823	34	7 月，拜倫離開義大利，去希臘加入反抗鄂圖曼帝國奴役的希臘獨立戰爭，擔任軍隊司令。
1824	35	過度的勞累和奔波使得他的身體健康惡化。4 月19 日，拜倫因治療無效病逝於希臘軍隊的軍帳中。臨終時，拜倫的遺囑寫道：「我的財產，我的精力都獻給了希臘的獨立戰爭，現在連生命也獻上吧！」此後希臘政府為拜倫舉行了隆重的國葬儀式。

拜倫詩選：漫步在美的光影/喬治.戈登.拜倫著；
陳金譯. -- 初版. -- 臺北市：笛藤出版圖書有限
公司, 2022.06
　　面；　公分
中英對照雙語版
譯自：She walks in beauty
ISBN 978-957-710-859-3(平裝)
873.51　　　　　　　　　111008468

2022年6月24日　初版第1刷　定價300元

著　　　者	喬治‧戈登‧拜倫
譯　　　者	陳　金
編　　　輯	江品萱
美 術 編 輯	王舒玕
總 編 輯	洪季楨
編 輯 企 劃	笛藤出版
發 行 所	八方出版股份有限公司
發 行 人	林建仲
地　　　址	台北市中山區長安東路二段171號3樓3室
電　　　話	(02) 2777-3682
傳　　　真	(02) 2777-3672
總 經 銷	聯合發行股份有限公司
地　　　址	新北市新店區寶橋路235巷6弄6號2樓
電　　　話	(02)2917-8022‧(02)2917-8042
製 版 廠	造極彩色印刷製版股份有限公司
地　　　址	新北市中和區中山路二段380巷7號1樓
電　　　話	(02)2240-0333‧(02)2248-3904
郵 撥 帳 戶	八方出版股份有限公司
郵 撥 帳 號	19809050

圖片來源：Unsplash